THE
WAITING
YEARS

FUMIKO ENCHI

Translated by JOHN BESTER

KODANSHA INTERNATIONAL
Tokyo • New York • London

Originally published by Kodansha Ltd. under the title *Onnazaka*.

Distributed in the United States by Kodansha America, Inc., 114 Fifth Avenue, New York, N.Y. 10011. Published by Kodansha International Ltd., 17-14 Otowa 1-chome, Bunkyo-ku, Tokyo 112, and Kodansha America, Inc. Copyright © 1971 by Kodansha International Ltd. All rights reserved. Printed in Japan.

LCC 72-158644
ISBN 0-87011-424-7
ISBN 4-7700-0794-9 (in Japan)

First paperback edition, 1980
92 93 94 95 16 15 14 13

1

First Bloom

It was an afternoon in early summer.

At the Kusumi's house that backed onto the Sumida River at Hanakawado in the Asakusa district of Tokyo, the mother, Kin, placed a white clematis from the garden in the alcove of one of the two adjoining rooms upstairs that she had been cleaning assiduously since early morning, and patting her hip with an air of weary finality came climbing down the dark wooden staircase.

In the small room next to the entrance hall, her daughter Toshi sat beneath the wooden-barred window threading a needle for her sewing, holding the eye up against the bright light reflected from the waters of the river. She spoke as her mother came into the room carrying the thick, oiled paper on which the flowers had rested while she arranged them.

"The clock next door just struck three. They're late, aren't they, Mother?"

"Good gracious, is it that time already? But then, they're coming all the way from Utsunomiya by rickshaw; they said afternoon but I expect it will be more like early evening."

Kin seated herself by the rectangular charcoal brazier and lit the tobacco in the tiny bowl of a longish, bamboo-stemmed pipe.

"You've been hard at it since this morning, Mother. I expect you're tired," said Toshi with a pleasant smile. She ran her sewing needle in and out of her double bun, which was coming slightly undone, then stuck it into the red pin cushion on the stitching stand. Next, she gently transferred her sewing—some material that looked like heavy silk crepe—from her lap to a piece of wrapping paper and went over to her mother, dragging her bad leg as she went. She too felt she deserved a rest.

"I wonder how it can get so dusty when I clean the place every day," said Kin, smoothing out her kimono sleeves that had been tied up for housework and fastidiously dusting off the black satin collar of her kimono with her hand. She did not mention it to her daughter, but she was secretly proud of having removed every speck of dust from the room, of having mounted a pair of steps even, so as to wipe the last traces of dust from the openwork panel over the lintel between the rooms and from the groove above the lintel itself.

"I wonder what Mrs. Shirakawa's coming up to Tokyo for," said Toshi, who was apparently less interested in the cleaning than her mother and was rubbing her eyes, which were tired from sewing, with her fingertips.

"What, exactly, are you hinting at?" Kin frowned suspiciously at her daughter. The mother was still youthful in outlook and the daughter had been prevented by sickness from marrying until it was too late, so that by now they were used to talking to each other more as sisters than as parent and child. Occasionally, even, Toshi seemed more elderly in her ideas than her mother.

"She said in her letter, didn't she, she was coming to Tokyo to do some sight-seeing?"

"Even so, I wonder." Toshi tilted her head portentously to one side. "I wonder whether a young married woman like her really has time to come up to Tokyo just to do the sights. Mr. Shirakawa's a chief secretary or something at the prefectural office, isn't he? Only just below the governor himself . . . "

"That's right. They say he's a very influential man," said Kin, tapping her pipe on the edge of the brazier. "Yes, he's certainly got on in the world. I never thought he'd do as well as that when he was working at the Tokyo City Hall and they lived next door to us. Not that he didn't have all his wits about him even then."

"That's just what I *mean*, Mother," said Toshi, as though urging her mother on. "It's all too casual, somehow, for her to leave a husband who's as busy as that and come up for a month or two of sightseeing, bringing her daughter and a maid and all. It isn't as though her own family lived here."

"You're right—she comes from Kumamoto, the same as Mr. Shirakawa himself. Even so, though . . . " Kin looked hard into her daughter's face as though the problem was beyond the grasp of her own imagination. "Surely they couldn't be thinking of a divorce? There was no hint of such a thing in Mr. Shirakawa's letter."

"I don't suppose there was," said Toshi. Her elbow rested on the covered end of the brazier, with her chin propped on her hand, and her eyes had a dreamy look as though gazing into the future. Even though Toshi was her own daughter, there were times when Kin was disturbed by the odd way that the crippled girl's presentiments had of coming true. For a while she gazed at Toshi's face with the air of one awaiting the utterance of a medium, but before long Toshi took her elbow off the brazier.

"There's no telling," she said.

It was an hour or so later that Tomo Shirakawa, accompanied by her nine-year-old daughter Etsuko and a maid, alighted from her rickshaw before the Kusumi's house.

First they went to the hot bath that was waiting and removed

9

the grime of their journey, then Tomo came back down to the sitting room to give them their presents: dried persimmons and Aizu lacquerware, which she said were local products of Fukushima, as well as lengths of cloth in suitable patterns for both Kin and Toshi.

Sitting there in her striped kimono, with the dignified loose jacket of black silk crepe decorated with the family crests, her sloping shoulders on which the clothes sat so well held slightly back, Tomo had the typical air of an important official's wife, an air acquired during the four or five years that Kin had not seen her. The breadth of her forehead and the generous spacing of her eyes and mouth about the well-shaped, somewhat fleshy nose saved her face from any suggestion of oversensitivity, but the eyes, narrow beneath the full, drooping eyelids, had an almost frustrated look, as though the lids were being used to screen off a whole variety of emotions that might have found expression there. It was this same heaviness of gaze, together with a certain formality of speech and manner, that had always made Kin, for one, sense a certain remoteness in Tomo, despite the cordiality that had developed during the two years or so that the Shirakawas had lived next door to them in Tokyo. There was no snobbishness, no unpleasantness, nothing one might censor; Kin, a typical Tokyo woman, would have expressed it by saying that Tomo "kept herself to herself." Yet now that her husband's position was more important than in his younger days, this same unbending quality in Tomo gave her an undeniable air of distinction.

Etsuko, whose hair was still too short to be done up properly and was fastened in a child's flat bun, was fascinated by the unfamiliar view of the river and could not keep her gaze off the barred window.

"She's getting to be a really beautiful girl," said Kin quite sincerely, so fair was Etsuko's complexion and so fine her features with the well-shaped, aquiline nose.

"She's like her father," added Toshi. It was true: the face with its graceful cheekline and the delicate set of the neck were more like Shirakawa himself than his wife. Etsuko seemed to fear the disapproval of her mother, who had only to utter the one word "Etsuko!" in a low voice for the girl to seem suddenly to shrink into herself and come to sit by her side.

"How nice that you could just up and come to Tokyo like this," said Kin as she bustled about making tea and serving it to them. "I hear your husband's an important figure these days, almost the same as the governor. It must be very wearing for you."

"Oh no, I know nothing about his official work nowadays . . . " She replied unaffectedly, with no trace of bragging or self-importance such as might confirm the talk Kin had heard of Mr. Shirakawa's living like a feudal lord in the prefecture where he worked.

For a while the talk flowed freely, chiefly of life in Tokyo: how certain areas were getting busy; how hairstyles had changed in the few years Tomo had been away; of the play they were doing now at the Shintomi Theater; till finally Tomo said, "And we're to enjoy ourselves this time without hurrying back . . . Though, to tell the truth, there *is* a little business mixed up with it too . . . " As she spoke, she turned to reset a red comb for Etsuko, who was by her side. So casual was the phrasing that Kin paid no attention, but to Toshi it meant that, as she herself had inferred, Tomo had some important business in Tokyo. Unruffled and gracious though Tomo's manner was, there seemed to be some unnatural burden weighing her down from within.

The next day Toshi, who was normally a stay-at-home, showed their gratitude for the presents they had received by asking Etsuko to go with her to visit the great temple of Kannon at Asakusa, and Yoshi the maid and Etsuko both set off happily in her company.

11

"On your way home, buy her a picture book or something at the arcade in front of the temple," Kin told her daughter as she went to the gate to see them off. Going indoors, she went straight upstairs where she found Tomo sitting in the anteroom, putting clothes into a wicker hamper that they had brought with them and taking out fresh ones. The sky with its scattered white clouds, reflected in the waters of the river below, filled the two rooms where Tomo sat with a spacious white light.

"Well—at work so soon?" exclaimed Kin, kneeling on the wooden floor of the veranda just outside the room.

"Now Etsuko's getting older she insists on taking this and that with her," said Tomo, speaking slowly as she put away kimonos one by one in the hamper. "It's made traveling anywhere quite a bother." She paused. "Mrs. Kusumi . . . I wonder if you're busy just at the moment?"

She had just leaned forward in order to put a yellow silk, lined kimono of Etsuko's deep down inside the hamper, and her face was not visible. It was precisely for the sake of a chat that Kin had come upstairs, but suddenly Tomo's words made her feel somehow awkward at having come up at all.

"No . . . Why, is there something I can do for you?"

"If you're busy, of course, it doesn't have to be now, but since Etsuko was out I thought . . . Either way, why don't you come in here for a while?"

Speaking in the same leisurely tone as ever, she brought a cushion and placed it on the *tatami* mats near the veranda.

"You see—to tell the truth, there's something I'd very much like you to do for me while I'm here."

"Now I wonder what that could be? If it's anything in my power I'll gladly do it, of course . . ."

Kin made a show of speaking heartily yet wondered desperately what Tomo was about to confide in her as she sat there so correctly with hands clasped in her lap and eyes downcast. The faintest of lines, like a very slight smile, extended from the edge of her gently curving cheek down to the corner of her mouth.

"It's a rather peculiar business, I'm afraid," she said, raising her hand to touch her sidelock. Hating even a single strand to be out of place, she had a habit of running a hand over her hair from time to time even though, in keeping with the whole of her personal appearance, it was always immaculately groomed.

At this point it dawned on Kin that, somewhere, a woman must be involved. When Shirakawa had been in Tokyo, women had always been coming to the house; it had worried Tomo, Kin knew, and now that he had reached his present position the likelihood of such an affair was all the greater. She deliberately maintained her inquiring expression nevertheless, since to probe into such a private matter as though she had already guessed its nature would have conflicted with her innate, townswoman's sense of etiquette.

"What is it? Don't hesitate to tell me," she said.

"Well, since I shall have to ask your help at any rate . . ." Again the smile, elusive as the smile on a Nō mask, played about the corners of Tomo's mouth.

"The fact is, you see, I'd like to find a maid to take back with me. Aged somewhere between fifteen and, say, seventeen or eighteen. From a respectable family, if possible . . . but she must be good-looking."

As she spoke the last words, the smile around her lips showed itself clearly, and the eyes beneath their heavy lids took on an intense light that went oddly with the smile.

"Of course, I quite understand."

Kin dropped her gaze, uncomfortable at the insincere ring of her own voice. She had already heard enough to justify the foreboding that Toshi had felt the other day.

13

She took a deep breath that might have been either a sign of assent or a sigh, then said:

"I suppose that when a man reaches his position . . . that kind of thing becomes a necessity, doesn't it?"

"It does seem so. People come to expect it, you see."

It was not true; with all her might, Tomo was checking the emotions that came welling up in her breast.

It was a year, perhaps, since her husband had first conceived the idea of taking a mistress into the house. The minor officials who danced attendance on Shirakawa had often bothered her with their innuendoes at saké parties and on other such occasions. "Mrs. Shirakawa," they would say, "with an establishment as big as this, you really ought to have more female help." Or, "The Chief Secretary has too much to do, you know. You should give him a little change now and then, he'll sleep a lot more soundly."

Her husband's failure to reprimand his subordinates for their impertinence, despite his usual strong distaste for such familiarity, gave Tomo the impression that he was using them in order to make the suggestion himself.

Familiar by now with Shirakawa's self-indulgence where women were concerned, Tomo could no longer feel for him the pure love she had experienced during the first few years of their marriage, yet his ability and his manly bearing still made him sufficiently attractive as a husband.

To take charge of a social life and household in keeping with her husband's present position had not been easy for a woman born into a low-ranking samurai family of the former Hosokawa clan and married early with no chance, in the social turmoil just preceding the Meiji Restoration, to acquire either a proper education or the usual social accomplishments of the well-bred young woman. Yet an inborn hatred of compromise made her impose upon herself a strict rule of conduct that gave first importance in everything to husband and family, and she supervised the daily affairs of their household with a meticulous care that was beyond criticism. All the love and wisdom of which she was capable were devoted to the daily lives of her husband and the rest of the Shirakawa family.

She seemed consequently old for her years. Though not a beauty, she was good-looking enough and more attentive than most women to her appearance, so that there was nothing particularly elderly about her, yet the innate strictness of disposition that made her take her responsibilities so seriously deprived her utterly of the ripe sensuality common in women of early middle age, and Shirakawa was astonished at times to find that a wife who in theory was ten years his junior should seem more like an elder sister. He was familiar of course with the fierce sensuality that burned with a low yet intense flame beneath the thick outer shell, and there were times when he himself felt a surge of warmth at the repressed passion he sensed within her, the passion that evoked so vividly the summer sun beating down mercilessly on the district of central Kyushu where she had been born and bred. One summer night, during the time when he was still working in Yamagata, a small snake had somehow got inside the mosquito net where he and his wife were sleeping. Wakening suddenly, he had felt something cold and wet at the front of his cotton night kimono. When he put his hand there, puzzled, the cold thing had started to slither away.

As he leapt to his feet with a cry, Tomo, startled, sat up sharply in bed. Drawing the lamp by the bed toward her and turning the light in his direction, she saw something like a slimy, shining black cord on her husband's shoulder.

Shirakawa's cry of "A snake!" and the movement of her hand as it stretched out automatically and grasped the living cord came simultaneously.

Half falling over Shirakawa, she went out to the veranda and threw the snake through the open shutters into the garden. She was trembling, yet in the breast that thrust through the gaping front of her kimono and in her bared arm he had sensed a robust directness that was normally shut away out of sight.

"Why did you throw it out? You should have let me kill it," he had complained, hating to give her the advantage. Even as he sensed the passionate nature within, he was beginning to find it difficult to see her as an object of desire. The strength that was a fraction greater than his own made him feel ill at ease in her presence.

"To call the girl a concubine would be making too much of it," he had said to Tomo. "She'll be a maid for you, too . . . It's a good idea, surely, to have a young woman with a pleasant disposition about the house so that you can train her to look after things for you when you're out calling. That's why I don't want to lower the tone of the household by bringing in a geisha or some other woman of that type. I trust you, and I leave everything to you, so use your good sense to find a young—as far as possible inexperienced—girl. Here, use this for your expenses."

He had set before her an astonishingly large sum of money.

Until then she had managed by pretending not to hear what others said, but there was no avoiding the issue now that Shirakawa himself had broached it with her. Should she refuse to accept the task it was almost certain that her husband would simply introduce into the family a woman chosen without consulting her. His leaving the choice to her was a sign of his trust, of the importance he attached, for the family's sake, to her position. A sense of this odd trust that was reposed in her had been there all the while, heavy in her heart, as she, with Yoshi and Etsuko, who felt nothing but joy at this chance to see the capital, sat swaying

16

in the rickshaws that had brought them all the way to the Ku-sumi's house in far-off Tokyo.

"I quite understand," said Kin. "There's a woman I'm friendly with who keeps a notion store and often acts as a go-between in this kind of thing, so I'll ask her right away."

Kin carried things forward on a businesslike basis, skillfully avoiding any direct reference to the private heaviness of Tomo's heart. Born into a family that had been official rice agents in Kuramac where the Shogun had his warehouses, Kin was well acquainted with the manners of the wealthier merchants and samurai of the old feudal era and was not in the least shocked by the idea that a man who had got on in the world should keep a concubine or even two. As she saw things, the jealousy of a wife in such a situation would be modified by a natural pride in such a sign of the family's increasing prosperity.

So it was that after Kin and her daughter were in bed that night, when Kin broached the subject, lowering her voice as though still constrained by Tomo's presence and with many glances up at the second floor, she was if anything surprised that her daughter should reply in a somber voice.

"Poor woman. You know, Mother—you say she's got more distinguished since we saw her last, but to me it looks like the distinction that comes through suffering. That first moment when our door opened and she came in, I got quite a shock."

"Oh well, people on whom fortune smiles always have their share of hard times too," said Kin lightly. "Anyway, I'd like to help her find some girl with a pleasant nature. It seems her hus-band told her that if she couldn't find a completely inexperienced girl a child geisha would do, just so long as she wasn't spoiled . . ."

Fresh from the official prefectural residence whose rooms were

17

hushed and chill like the priests' quarters of some great temple, the child Etsuko was captivated by the second floor of this house that was so cheerful, with its broad view directly over the waters of the Sumida River and its sounds of creaking rudders and lapping waves that came to the ears all day long. When Toshi was busy, she would go out through the back gate onto the quay and watch the gentle motion of the water lapping at the stakes beneath her feet, or listen entranced to the stirring cries of the boatmen as they busily rowed their loaded vessels by. On one such occasion, Toshi's pale face peered out through the bars of the window and she called:

"Mind you don't fall, Miss Etsuko." Today as usual Tomo was out with Kin.

"I'm all right," Etsuko called, turning round with a smile. She was charming, with her regular features and oval face that looked so grown-up for its age, and the small topknot tied with its crimson cloth.

"Come along," said Toshi, "I've got something nice for you."

"Coming," Etsuko replied obediently and walked over to the window, the long red-striped sleeves of her kimono fluttering in the breeze as she went. Beneath the bars of the window, twining around slender bamboo sticks, grew the five or six morning glories that Kin tended so lovingly, coaxing them carefully from the tiny plot of soil. Seen from outside, both Toshi's face at the window and the sewing spread out on her lap seemed to Etsuko somehow different from when she saw them indoors. Toshi put a thin arm through the bars and dangled before Etsuko's eyes the stuffed monkey of red silk that she held between her fingers.

"Isn't it pretty!" Clinging to the bars with both hands, Etsuko gazed happily at the tiny monkey on its string, her smile so unclouded that Toshi reflected with a knowing nod to herself that the child did not miss its mother.

18

"Where's your mummy gone?" she asked, jiggling the monkey up and down on its string.

"She's gone to see somebody," said Etsuko in a clear voice.

"I expect you miss your mother, don't you dear?"

"Yes," she replied, but her eyes were lively and unclouded as she added, "but then I've got Yoshi."

"Yes, of course—there's Yoshi, isn't there," said Toshi with a nod. "Is your mummy very busy even when she's at home?"

"Yes," said Etsuko in the same clear voice as before. "People come to see us."

"Dear me! And is your daddy out a lot?"

"Yes, he's at the prefectural office all day. And at night he's often invited out, or people come to see him, so quite often I don't see him once all day."

"I see . . . And how many maids do you have?"

"Three. Yoshi, Seki, and Kimi. And then we have a steward and a houseboy."

"Well, you *do* have a big family, don't you? It's no wonder Mummy's so busy."

Toshi stopped her sewing and a smile spread over her face. She was picturing to herself the woman that Tomo would find during her present stay and take home with her, and imagining the changes that she might bring to Etsuko's life.

Around the same time that Toshi and Etsuko were talking to each other, Tomo and Kin were engaged in conversation with a male geisha called Zenkō on the second floor of a riverside teahouse in the geisha district of Yanagibashi.

Kin was treating Tomo as though she were her mistress and effacing herself completely. Zenkō, a dapper man who having started life in the family of a retainer of the Shogun knew how to relax without becoming ingratiating, spoke to his old acquaintance

Kin in a tone free of the mannerisms of his trade often associated.

"Well now, from what I've just heard, I should say it will be quite difficult. Still, we have four or five quite personable girls coming in a little while."

He twirled his slender silver pipe between his fingers as though not quite sure what to do with it. Privately, he was wondering with disgust just what part of the provinces had produced the kind of man who would have his legal wife search for a concubine for him. It confirmed his dislike for provincials in general, yet as he sat facing Tomo he sensed something in her manner that seemed somehow to match the pride in tradition still surviving in himself, something that was neither proud nor ingratiating, that was not in the slightest out of the ordinary yet suggested an old-fashioned formality that could not be sneered at or made fun of.

"After all, even with someone *we* might think is all right, you never can tell a gentleman's taste, can you?" said Kin, a ready talker, glancing at Tomo as she returned to Zenkō the cup that he had filled with saké for her.

"Come now," protested Zenkō, "you mustn't rely too much on my judgment. Take these girl students nowadays, for instance, with their hair cut straight across the front and their foreign-style parasols. Myself, I just can't . . ."

"Now, now, Mr. Hosoi, the lady's not looking for a girl to act as mistress for some foreigner. Anyway, I'm sure that if you looked among the child geishas you'd still be able to find a girl with the old *ukiyo-e*-style beauty that you like."

"No—the trouble with me is that I say what I think, and the young girls won't have anything to do with me."

As he finished speaking a patter of feet sounded on the stairway leading up from the second floor, a medley of voices chimed in greetings, and four or five apprentice geishas in the charge of an elderly geisha came into the room.

20

"Are we late?" the elderly geisha said to Zenkō, beginning without delay to tune a samisen that a maid handed to her.

The story had been that the wife of an official in the provinces wanted to see a colorful dance by apprentice geishas as something to remember Tokyo by, and the girls were decked out in the gay finery that they would not normally have worn for a daytime engagement.

The preliminary piece of instrumental music over, the young geishas took turns dancing in pairs. Those who were not dancing came to wait on Tomo and her companions, fetching and removing dishes of food and pouring out saké for them. Tomo, who disliked saké, raised her cup to her lips from time to time in order to give her hands something to do as she watched the dancers and the young geishas who sat near her in conversation with Zenkō and Kin.

They must have been aged about fourteen or fifteen. There were two of them who formed a strikingly beautiful pair, yet as they were dancing, one exposed an arm that was thin, dark-skinned and undernourished, while the other had lines at the sides of her sharp nose that showed when she laughed in a way that was brutal and made her look like a heron. The mere idea of such a girl gradually growing to maturity in their family was a chilling prospect, and for the first time Tomo felt almost grateful that her husband had left the choice to her.

After the young geishas had gone, she told Kin what she felt about them.

"You certainly have a good eye," broke in Zenkō before Kin could reply. Kin herself, who during the past few days had been helping Tomo in assessing all kinds of girls, had sometimes found herself more alarmed than impressed by the sensitivity and acuity of Tomo's judgment. It startled her to find that a woman who in normal social situations had never talked critically of others nor shown much positive interest should be able, when the occasion required, to make such a thorough-going appraisal of other women.

It had been the same with the girl that Oshigi the haberdasher had brought along. Quiet-spoken with good, regular features, she was the kind of girl that Kin would have jumped at, but Tomo shook her head.

"They said she was sixteen," she declared with seeming reluctance, "but she's at least eighteen. Besides, you know, I don't think she's quite inexperienced."

Kin was skeptical, but on further inquiry discovered that the girl had indeed had an affair with her elder sister's husband, a craftsman.

"I wonder how you can tell?" said Kin, gazing wonderingly at Tomo, who dropped her eyes as though embarrassed at her own accomplishment.

"I wasn't always like this," she said, heaving a sigh as though in deprecation of her present self. It seemed that she had acquired the ability to see through to a woman's true self in the course of witnessing Shirakawa's various affairs. Kin was not usually one to bother herself too deeply with the preoccupations and tribulations of others, but little by little as she accompanied Tomo in her search for a concubine she seemed to divine the nature of that "distinction acquired through suffering" of which her daughter Toshi had spoken.

Tomo was sitting by the night table looking through a pile of photographs of beautiful women when Etsuko came up silently and looked over her shoulder.

"What pretty people! Who are they, Mummy?" she asked, the red cloth on her hair tilting inquisitively to one side. Tomo did not reply but gave Etsuko a few of the photographs and said,

"Etsuko, which do *you* like best?"

"Now let me see . . ." said Etsuko fanning the photographs out in her hand.

"This one," she intoned in her child's voice, and pointed to the middle photograph. It was a half-portrait, done against a white background, of a girl of fourteen or fifteen with her hair done up high in a style then popular among young girls and her arms tightly folded. The forehead with its conical hairline like Mt. Fuji and the strikingly large eyes like half-shaded spheres of black jade had awoken a response in Etsuko's childish mind.

"I see. You too . . . ," said Tomo as though surprised, and taking the photograph she gazed at it again.

"Tell me, Mummy. Who is it?"

"It doesn't matter, you'll know soon," said Tomo as she gathered the photos together again.

The photograph had arrived a few days previously from Zenkō Sakuragawa, the male geisha at Yanagibashi.

The task of selection that faced Tomo was difficult. She had already been at Kin's for more than a month yet still no girl worth telling Shirakawa about had come to light. Several times she had written to her husband in her labored hand explaining that under no circumstances did she wish to bring back someone who did not please him, and each time the reply from Shirakawa had said that there was no hurry; she was to give every care to her choice. Nevertheless, as the rainy season gave way to clear skies and the Bon Festival drew near Tomo began to feel a sense of urgency. Not only her husband but the home, left without its mistress were weighing heavily on her conscience.

It was at this point that the new proposal had come from Zenkō. This time, Kin had been told, Mrs. Shirakawa was quite certain to be satisfied.

The girl was called Suga and was fifteen years old; her father owned a shop that sold bamboo skin for wrapping purposes. Her accomplishments included the Nishikawa style of dancing, which she had been studying since she was a small child. She was an attractive girl and since early childhood had won applause whenever she appeared in performances put on by her dancing school. The mother and the elder brother, who was now head of the family, were both reputable citizens, but a dishonest employee had been into the firm during the past few years and the family had fallen on hard times. They had been driven to a point where they would either have to dispose of the shop or sell the girl to a geisha house. The mother had had no idea of making her a rich man's concubine, but the dancing teacher, who was on friendly terms with Zenkō, had heard of Shirakawa and decided to mention the matter to him, thinking that it might better serve the girl's own future interests to be taken into such a distinguished family than to be set adrift in the uncertain world of the geisha.

"She's a quiet girl," the dancing teacher had said. "And another thing is she's unusually fair-skinned for a Tokyo girl. When she goes to the public bath the children actually come over to stare at her."

In a few days' time the pupils of the school were to give a recital at which the girl called Suga would dance "Plum Blossom in Spring," so on that day Tomo and Kin set off for the teacher's house with Zenkō leading the way. On the pretext of going to see the recital, they were to take a covert look at the girl. The teacher's house stood in a narrow alley tucked away among the houses of the wholesale merchants of Kokuchō. The front it presented to the street was narrow, but upstairs there was a stage, and when Tomo and the others went up a small girl was already dancing a piece called "Gorō" to the accompaniment of the teacher's samisen.

Seeing Zenkō, the teacher without pausing in her playing gave an almost imperceptible nod and smiled briefly, the dark hollow of her mouth with its black-dyed teeth throwing her lively-looking eyes into still greater prominence.

They had calculated the approximate time of their arrival so that Suga should be present, and the three of them glanced with affected unconcern around the girls who were jammed into the tiny room watching the stage. All of them wore cotton summer kimonos with sashes mostly of red, but one girl, sitting at the far side totally absorbed in the dancing, told them at once by her outstanding beauty that this was Suga. She sat still and correct, little affected by the heat it seemed, while the others about her busily plied their fans.

Her build was large for a girl of fifteen but the features were unmistakably those in the photographs. The soft white texture of the skin, like handmade paper, and the hair with its blue sheen that framed the pale face in almost oppressive profusion threw the eyebrows and eyes into even sharper prominence, giving them a dramatic beauty as though she were made up for the stage.

Tomo gazed at Suga with a sense almost of shock. The girl was beautiful, that was all: nothing in the expression remotely suggested any spiritual depths. But the impression of purity was undeniable. Her voice as she spoke to her companion was subdued; she would say something with downcast gaze then listen to the other's reply with eyes wide open in a way that was natural and unaffected.

When "Gorō" came to an end, the teacher handed the samisen to her assistant and said, "You next, Suga," then rose and came over to where Tomo and the others were sitting.

The girl who rose to her feet and, lifting the hem of her kimono with both hands, walked towards the stage stooping modestly as she went, was indeed the girl whom Tomo's gaze had singled out.

"That's her," said the teacher easily to Tomo and Kin as the first notes of the samisen broke the silence. "A really sweetnatured girl; I'm sure you'll have no trouble at all in training her."

As they watched Suga going through the movements of the dance, the teacher broke in from time to time with details of her background. For all her striking looks, she was so retiring by nature that even though she was quick to learn, her dancing somehow lacked sparkle. She had no taste for showing off her skills in front of others and had acquired the feminine accomplishments principally to please her parents, declaring that a placid type of person like herself would never make a success in such a lively occupation as that of geisha. The busy town did not really suit her nature, and she felt sure that she would feel much lighter in spirit if she lived in some tranquil spot with a broad view of green paddies and streams. Suga's mother, the teacher said, was a devoted parent. When she had first heard about Shirakawa from the teacher and been told that Suga would have to go to Fukushima, the idea of her daughter's going so far away had reduced her to tears; if they were pleased with the girl and decided to take her on, she had said, she must meet the wife and have a thorough talk with her, since so much in her daughter's future would depend on how the wife felt about the situation.

Most of this conversation took place between Zenkō and Kin. Tomo's eyes were fixed on Suga's dancing but she took in enough of their talk to convince her more surely than in any other case so far of the depth of the mother's affection for her daughter. The daughter of such a mother was unlikely to have been seriously spoiled by the world, and promised to respond readily to Tomo's instruction if she took her back with her to Fukushima.

Even in her dancing, although Tomo was no good judge, the movements of eyes and limbs had a vaguely subdued quality that robbed it of brilliance despite its skill. This, again, did not displease Tomo. Almost without realizing it, she had conceived an antipathy to any suggestion of a clearcut, strong personality in the woman who was to intrude on her household. A girl with strikingly young, fresh features but a spirit that was subdued and timid—for Tomo, it was almost the ideal type for the "second woman" in the house.

"Don't you think she looks promising?" asked Zenkō as soon as they emerged from the narrow side street on their way home. "She's not made to be a geisha," he went on. "Girls with that introspective air aren't popular."

"Are you really sure?" asked Kin doubtfully. "And her so pretty . . ."

"Looks alone aren't enough," he said. "But remember—that's the kind of woman that in ten years' time will firm up wonderfully. That's the one thing you should be concerned with."

"Yes, you may be right." A shiver ran over Tomo's skin as though it had been touched by the naked blade of a sword. The same tremor had passed over her from time to time as she had watched Suga dance.

As she gazed at the innocent body of this girl who, for all the provocative movements—the inclinations of the head and the elusive movements of the body—with which she suggested the amorous affairs of men and women on the stage, was in fact still half a child, Tomo found herself wondering in what way this immature girl would be broken in, how she would be transformed, once they took her to their home, and delivered her into the practiced hands of Shirakawa; unconsciously she closed her eyes and held her breath, only to see a vision of her husband and Suga with limbs intertwined that brought the blood rushing to her head and made her open her eyes wide again as though to dispel a nightmare. Pity welled up at the sorry fate of the girl fluttering before her like a great butterfly, and with it a jealousy that flowed about her body in a rapid, scorching stream.

Her mind that under the pressure of the search had felt nothing so long as no suitable woman had presented herself was suddenly assailed with a yearning like the hunger that comes with the ending of a fast. The pain of having publicly to hand over her husband to another gnawed at her within. To Tomo, a husband who would quite happily cause his wife such suffering was a monster of callousness. Yet since to serve her husband was the creed around which her life revolved, to rebel against his outrages would have been to destroy herself as well; besides, there was the love that was still stronger than that creed. Tormented by the one-sided love that gave and gave with no reward, she had no idea, even so, of leaving him. It was true that Shirakawa's money and property, their daughter Etsuko, and their son Michimasa now living with relatives in the country were bonds that held her, but still stronger was the longing, whatever the sacrifice, to have her husband understand through and through the innermost desires and emotions of her heart. The longing was something that no one other than Shirakawa could fulfill.

At the idea of another woman, this young girl Suga, coming between herself and her husband, it seemed to Tomo that the husband with whom even in the past she had never been able to effect real contact was moving still farther away.

The night after she received his reply conveying approval of the photograph of Suga that she had sent, Tomo dreamed that she killed her husband and woke in fright at the sound of her own cry.

Even after she awoke, the force that had gone into her hands to strangle him was still vividly apparent in her clenched fists; she sat up in bed appalled at herself and stayed for a while hugging her body with her arms.

Etsuko's face as she lay on her side sleeping soundly in the bed next to Tomo's stood out in pale profile in the light from the low wick of the bedside lamp. Tomo felt a pang of love for the innocence of the sleeping face that formed so striking a contrast with its comparatively grownup expression when she was awake. So alert was Tomo to the danger of spoiling her that Etsuko tended to find her affection elsewhere, attaching herself more to maids and other friendly adults than to her mother; little did she imagine how Tomo now, wakening in the small hours from a dream of horror, lay bathed in sweat, gazing with tearful eyes at her daughter as though she were a solitary spring in a scorching desert.

On the day that Suga and her mother came to the Kusumi's to meet them for the first time, Etsuko, who had been told by her mother and Kin that they would be taking Suga back to Fukushima with them, seemed captivated in her childish way with Suga's beauty.

"Isn't she pretty?" she said. "She's the girl in the photo, isn't she? What's she going to do at home?"

"She's going to help your father," said Tomo, momentarily averting her eyes.

"You mean, like Seki?"

"Yes . . . Yes, I suppose so."

Etsuko fell silent, sensing that she would be scolded if she inquired further. Yoshi also, who had been sternly bidden to silence by Tomo, said nothing to her about Suga.

However complex her emotions, Tomo was obliged to keep them hidden while interviewing Suga's mother. The mother, who unlike Suga was small with a snub nose and round face, clearly felt intense guilt towards Suga at letting her go for the sake of money, and talked in great detail to Tomo as to one who was her only source of hope, telling her how Suga was not strong physically and even confiding that she was "not really a woman" yet.

"But now I feel much better," she said to Kin, "seeing what a kind, decent mistress she'll have. The lady says that even if the master turns against Suga in the future, she'll be sure to look after her interests."

As she watched Suga's mother telling Kin all this in her own presence and with such näive confidence in her, Tomo resolved in her own mind that she would never let harm come to Suga. She must be responsible for everything, even the future security of the woman who was presumably to deprive her of her husband's love. Occasionally she would smile a lonely smile at the irony of her lot. At such times she could slip free of the bonds in which she was entangled and, however briefly, survey herself and her husband, Suga and Etsuko, with the same dispassionate gaze.

One morning two or three days after the Bon Festival, Tomo's party with the addition of Suga left the Kusumi's in four rickshaws.

Suga in her purple splash-patterned kimono of thin silk with its sash of heavy Hakata silk rode the first part of the way in the same rickshaw as Etsuko, who was reluctant to be separated from her.

"The young lady's taken a fancy to her, too," said Kin as she and her daughter went back to the living room after seeing off the rickshaw with its burden that was so like two colorful blossoms, one large and one small. "That's *something* to be thankful for."

She took off the apron she had been wearing and glanced at her daughter as she folded it up. Toshi walked over to the bow window, her bad leg dragging as she went.

"That Mr. Shirakawa is a wicked man, isn't he?" she said. "I felt so sorry for all three of them—the mistress and the young lady, and Suga—that I cried . . ."

She dabbed at the corner of her eyes with her fingers as she tucked the stitching stand between her knees.

Green Grapes

At one time it had been the inn where visiting feudal lords always stayed. Even today the Kamisuya, where two guests sat facing each other across a *go* board by the balcony of a second-story room whose green bamboo blinds were rolled up to let in a cool breeze, was the best inn in Utsunomiya and the destination of all prominent visitors. In the better of the two seats sat Yukitomo Shirakawa, Chief Secretary at the prefectural office of the neighboring prefecture of Fukushima. His companion was a minor official called Ōno who had come in attendance on him. Shirakawa was the right-hand man of Michiaki Kawashima, one of the driving forces behind the government of the day and a man so feared in his own prefecture that mere mention of the "demon governor," it was said, was enough to silence a crying child. He was a leader too in the governor's drive to wipe out the civil rights movement that had begun to rear its head so frequently of late.

Shirakawa was thin, so thin that the summer kimono of linen with the narrow band of light blue showing below his long, slender neck billowed out with an effect of coolness. His nose was aquiline in an oval face, and his eyes, despite the mild expression with which he habitually veiled them, would from time to time dart a fierce light that suggested more than a trace of monomania. Yet at first glance he was merely a middle-aged gentleman of a neat and unassuming appearance that seemed to belie his position as chief henchman of the "demon governor."

31

"They're late, surely?" said Ōno as he swept toward him the black stones that he had been using in the game just finished. Shirakawa took a puff at the tobacco in his silver pipe, then without haste drew out the gold watch tucked beneath his sash and said, half to himself:

"It's getting on to five—I imagine they'll be here soon. The steward's gone to the outskirts of the town to meet them, so they can hardly miss the way."

He affected composure, but the eagerness with which he was waiting was betrayed by the fact that he did not suggest another game. Ōno moved the *go* board out of the way and glanced at the *tatami* where it had stood to make sure there was no dust; he knew how fastidious Shirakawa was about such things.

Shirakawa, who had arrived in this town the day before on the pretext of a need to visit the prefectural office of Tochigi prefecture, had in reality come to await the wife and daughter whom he had sent to Tokyo more than three months previously. Ōno had already heard from the Shirakawas' steward, who had accompanied them, that it was something more than a desire to meet his daughter and his wife of such long standing that had brought him all the way to Utsunomiya.

"They say she's a terrific beauty," the steward had declared with a sensational air. "Either way, the master's a queer one, sending his wife all the way to Tokyo to choose her for him." He looked scandalized.

Ōno had already heard occasional reports of Shirakawa's ways —how the governor had remarked that if Shirakawa was going to carry on as he did it would be better for his family if he kept a concubine or two at home; how he was going to become the patron of some geisha or other in Fukushima—but being, like the steward, a conventional man himself, the idea of a wife going to Tokyo and using her own judgment in finding a concubine to bring home

32

astonished him. He wondered, in the first place, how a respectable woman like Shirakawa's wife had ever set about finding a woman suitable as a concubine in a place as big as Tokyo. Could it be that a woman married to a man of great worldly ambition herself developed talents beyond the imagination of men such as himself?

Suddenly there were sounds of rickshaws drawing up before the entrance downstairs, followed by a confused murmur of men's and women's voices greeting newly arrived guests and the sound of footsteps hurrying along corridors.

"Here they are, I think," said Ōno, who got hastily to his feet and made for the staircase at a trot.

It was one hour or so later that Shirakawa's wife Tomo led forward a fresh, unspoiled-looking young girl with her hair drawn back in a bun and said:

"This is Suga, who has come back with me to enter the family service."

Earlier, Tomo and Etsuko had greeted Shirakawa briefly while Suga waited downstairs, then Tomo had sent Suga to have a bath with Etsuko. When she came back, she had seated her in front of the mirror-stand and combed out her sidelocks and bun for her. Suga's hair after the bath gleamed like black lacquer; it was heavy and hard to comb, but Tomo found herself marveling anew at the dazzling fairness of the face without makeup that was framed by the glossy black locks. Since she had used her own judgment in selecting the girl and had given the mother a considerable sum of money in exchange, she must now convince her husband with his acute eye for feminine beauty that she had found a great bargain that should not have been missed, and she worked to make the beautiful Suga seem still more beautiful, watching with strangely mixed feelings as Etsuko romped innocently about them, peering at Suga in the mirror as though at a large doll and exclaiming:

33

"I like hair ornaments, they're pretty."

"I'm very inexperienced, sir, but I hope I shall give satisfaction."

The shoulders in the purple silk kimono with the girlish shoulder-tucks seemed to shrink together as Suga, kneeling and bowing low to the floor, stumbled through the greeting in precisely the form that her mother in Tokyo had taught her. A young girl of fifteen sacrificed for the sake of her family's fortunes, her only instructions were that she would be going into service for life with the Shirakawa family in Fukushima. She was to wait on the master as his maid, but as to the nature of the service she had been told nothing. The one thing she dreaded above all was a reprimand, being resolved all her days to observe her mother's solemn injunction that she look after her master well and never disobey his wishes whatever might happen. Luckily, she had struck up a friendship with the nine-year-old daughter Etsuko during their two or three days together in Tokyo, and the mistress too, she was relieved to find, was in no way an unkind person despite the formality typical of people from the provinces. That left only the most important person of all, the master, who was certain to be an awesome figure since he was far older, it seemed, than his wife and, as chief secretary or some such important-sounding position in the prefecture, sometimes stood in for the governor himself. Whatever would she do if he were to scold her in a loud voice? In Tokyo, there would at least have been a home she could run back to, but the thought of such a thing happening in Fukushima untold scores of miles away made her unutterably wretched . . .

" 'Suga,' eh? A good name. Tell me, how old are you?"

"Fifteen, sir."

She replied for all she was worth, then sat with tense features as though she might burst into tears at any moment. With the

34

straight lines of her unnaturally thick eyebrows contracted very slightly and the sharply defined lids of her large eyes wide open as though in surprise, her face in the yellowish light of the lamp was sharply etched like an actor's on the stage. Shirakawa was reminded of the extraordinary facial beauty of a well-known courtesan called Imamurasaki, seen long ago one night in cherry-blossom time, parading with her retinue through Yoshiwara.

"You must find it lonely here in the country after a busy place like Tokyo?"

"Oh no, sir."

"Do you like Kabuki?"

"Yes, sir," she replied and went rigid with doubt lest this had not been the right thing to say.

"Just like Tomo," he said laughing. "We have a theater here in Fukushima, you know. I believe an Osaka actor called Tokizō is playing there at the moment, so I'll take you as soon as we get back."

Although the master was in a good mood, each mild phrase he uttered fell on Suga's ears with hidden menace.

It was not until he had dismissed her with a "You'd better get a good night's sleep" and she had gone from the room with Etsuko still following that the stiffness left her body and she relaxed.

"I'm afraid she seems to have a rather retiring nature," said Tomo hesitantly with a glance at her husband's face as they watched Suga leaving the room. Beneath the drooping lids, Shirakawa's eyes had a gleam like light on dark restless waters. It was the expression he always wore when he felt attracted by a desirable woman. Time and again the overwhelmingly joyful experiences of Tomo's younger years had turned sour as she was forced to watch with a helpless horror, as though her very flesh and blood were being devoured by maggots, while her husband's eyes lighted on another woman in just this way.

"Why? She looks gentle, surely that's a good thing? I'm sure a girl like that will make a perfectly good companion for Etsuko."

His tone was impersonal, but his gaze had followed intently the innocent, childlike movement of Suga's hips as, clutching at her long sleeves, she rose abruptly to her feet and left the room. The movement, like a boy's in its innocence of female sexuality, was precisely that of the Tomo whom his mother had invited to their house in the country at the age of fourteen. The discovery excited Shirakawa all the more in that Suga's face, shoulders and breasts had a rounded, ample, feminine air. He had asked Tomo particularly to find a girl as unspoilt and unsophisticated as possible, the kind of girl who would do equally well as her own maid, but now he was almost ashamed that she had respected his wishes so carefully, searching so diligently to find this flower in the bud whose petals were even more tightly folded than he had dared to hope.

"You say her parents have a bamboo-wrapper shop?"

"Yes, in Kokuchō. They used to have quite a good business, but apparently they had a dishonest employee, and the business went downhill. I met the mother; she seemed an extremely pleasant, straightforward person."

At this point it occurred to Tomo that she should talk to Shirakawa about the enormous sum of money with which he had entrusted her to pay for the search. She had used five hundred yen to pay Suga's family and buy her new clothes; before finding Suga she had also spent money engaging apprentice geishas and in interviewing via intermediaries several girls of non-professional or semi-professional standing; but even after this more than one half of the money her husband had given her still remained in her keeping. She had intended to return it to Shirakawa immediately she arrived at the inn. Once more now she tried to turn to the subject yet for some reason the words seemed suddenly to stick in her throat and nothing came to her lips. She flushed in a kind of panic, but Shirakawa, who seemed to notice nothing, clapped his hands to summon Ōno.

"Ōno—let's finish the game we started. We'll be up early tomorrow morning, so Tomo had better go to bed early downstairs."

Tomo got up to go, with a sidelong view as she did so of Ōno's short frame straining over the *go* board that he was carrying out to the center of the room. She was thirty, and the fact that her husband, whose eyes tonight had an intensity that gave him a new appeal, should make no move towards her tormented her spiritually and physically all the more after a separation of three months. Whether the torment that seethed within her was love or hatred she could not tell, but a calm determination not to leave the crucible of doubt gave her features the tranquillity of a Nō mask in her unhurried progress along the corridor.

To Suga's eyes, reared as she was in Tokyo, the streets of Fukushima were half deserted; even the shelves of the shops on the main streets looked half empty and uninviting. Shirakawa's official residence was at a place called Yanagi Koji some six hundred yards from the prefectural office. It was a former samurai's residence with a long, roofed gateway, and its verandas, high like those of a temple, skirted large rooms each ten or twelve *tatami* mats in size. In the back garden, beyond the ever-open sliding doors of the back rooms, an orchard of persimmon, apple, and pear trees and grapevines grew in a profusion of green next to a field of vegetables.

The first shock awaiting Tomo on her return to their residence was a new wing to the house, three rooms emitting a fragrance of new cedarwood and entirely surrounded by a veranda, that stood in a sunny location facing south just in front of the vines in the orchard. The rooms were connected to the main building of the house by a covered passageway.

"The carpenters came not long after you'd gone," said Seki the housemaid, with an overwrought expression. That Seki's relationship with Shirakawa had been something more than that between servant and master Tomo had once learned indirectly from Seki herself.

Going into the new wing, Tomo was astonished to find a new mulberry-wood mirror-stand with a bright crimson cover of crepe over the glass and a chest-of-drawers standing ostentatiously in the six-*tatami* dressing room.

"New quilts, too," said Seki with a look of acute discomfort, opening the closet to show Tomo. Inside, two new sets of well-padded bedding in heavy yellow checkered silk, one in the upper compartment and one in the lower, lay on wrapping cloths of silk dyed in a pattern of fresh twining greenery, cozily trailing the sleeves of their patterned-silk, padded covers.

"Whose room is this?" asked Etsuko, who had followed them in, tilting to one side as she spoke the fair-skinned, oval face that was so like Shirakawa's.

"Your father had it built for reading his official papers in. Now go away dear," said Tomo sharply as though repelling her. Above all, she must not let this thing that threatened to engulf her whole existence become a threat to her daughter as well. To Etsuko, however, this desperate determination merely made her mother seem forbidding. She liked much better to be with someone pretty like Suga, who seemed to give off a pleasant fragrance when you went near her; and she ran off willingly along the corridor.

"Should I put the master's bed out in here from tonight?" asked Seki, her eyes seeming to bore into Tomo as she spoke.

"Yes, you'd better."

"And Miss Suga in the anteroom?"

"We'll leave Suga to get out her own bed."

Though Tomo's outward manner was dignified and pleasant, she shifted her gaze to the garden, overcome by an unbearable sense of shame at the idea that the same fierce fire burned in Seki's breast as in her own.

She could see Suga and Etsuko standing face to face beneath the serrated leaves of the grapevine in the orchard. Suga, in a cotton kimono with a pattern in white on dark blue, had her hand, probably at Etsuko's insistence, stretched above her head, clutching lightly at a bunch of green grapes that hung above her. The sunlight falling through the vine flecked the fair skin of her face with green.

"Can you eat them as green as this?"

"They're very good. They're a kind of green grape they grow in Western countries."

Etsuko's voice came cool and clear. Suga pulled off the bunch and placed one of the grapes like a great green gem in her mouth.

"I told you so—it's sweet, isn't it? The agricultural testing station next door gave the vine to us."

"Well, so it is! I've never had a green grape like this that was so sweet."

Smiling at each other happily the two girls plucked the grapes and conveyed them to their coral lips. Seen like this Suga, so big and grown-up when she was on her best behavior indoors, was still no more than an innocent playmate for Etsuko. Yet even as Tomo's eyes watched the girl's innocent, childlike features, smiling as though with a sense of release, and the relaxed movements of the limbs, the image of the yellow silk bedding in the closet just behind her bore down oppressively on her mind and refused to go away.

It was wicked. They were giving a girl still of an age to be playing with dolls to a man a full two dozen years her senior, an elderly roué who had already tasted all the world's pleasures. The girl's parents were a party to the whole proceedings. Even if they had not given her to be his mistress, they could never have got enough money to keep the family going without handing over her fresh young body in exchange. Her physical beauty was so dazzling that her unspoiled charms would have been destined to be ravished, sooner or later, if not here then somewhere else; even so, much as the throat rebels at the idea of swallowing in cold blood the flesh of a bird killed before one's eyes, Tomo felt a vague sense of guilt, shared with her husband, for having gone to buy Suga. Why must she contribute to this cruelty that was little better than slave-trading?

As she watched Suga, with the cool skin that harbored an inner light like newly fallen snow and the dewy eyes that were always wide open yet had a misleadingly troubled look, Tomo would experience two unbidden and conflicting emotions: boundless pity as for a charming animal that was about to be led to the slaughter, and fixed hatred at the thought that eventually this innocent girl might turn into a devil that would devour her husband and sweep unchecked through the whole house.

The day following their return to Fukushima a man from Marui's, the family drapers, began to appear in the living room almost every day, bringing with him great bundles of cloth. He usually came after Shirakawa was back from the prefectural office, so that the master could glance through the cloths of many colors spread about the spacious room and make the choice himself. He bought clothes for Tomo and Etsuko as well, but the real purpose of course was to buy a complete outfit for Suga.

As though buying a trousseau for a bride, he bought every kind of garment she was likely to need, from formal black kimonos with the family crest and a colored pattern around the bottom of the skirt only, to sashes of figured satin, fine gauze-like silks, linen, striped crepe, and even the long red undergarments.

Finding herself, a newcomer, providing no service but treated instead as a guest, Suga was less pleased than perplexed that clothes should be made for her in this way. But at such times the gleam in Shirakawa's eyes that was like a light moving on dark waters would grow stronger. "Suga," he would say, a pink flush suffusing his thin cheeks as it did when he was angry, his eyes gleaming with an unnaturally bright light, "put this purple over your shoulder and stand there with the spotted sash against it to see how they match."

She would slip the half-finished kimono over her shoulders timidly, half uncomfortably yet with the practiced air of a tradesman's daughter who was used to wearing dancing costume, then she would hold the spotted sash round it at the front and stand there, as vivid and attractive as a woman in one of Kobayashi Kiyochika's brightly colored portraits. The maids and the man from Marui's who sat watching would give an involuntary exclamation of admiration. Most delighted of them all, Etsuko would go over to stand by Suga and exclaim, "Oh, it's so pretty!" Fair-skinned and slender as a young crane, Etsuko looked more refined than ever when she stood by the unopened peony that was Suga. It was yet another source of satisfaction to Shirakawa.

"A pattern of vetch on a white ground will be best for Etsuko," he would say, turning round to Tomo, "with a satin sash to go with it."

Shirakawa's unaccustomed animation and Suga's complete lack of bashfulness towards him despite her timidity told Tomo that so far he had made no physical advances towards her. In order to possess himself of a girl more than twenty years his junior even Shirakawa, it seemed, was obliged to employ a technique completely different from when he made advances to geishas or maids. To clothe a girl from a poor family in the most luxurious garments possible was in itself almost certainly a means of winning Suga's heart. Watching him from the corner of her eye, Tomo remembered the husband who had once so carefully selected hair ornaments, neckbands and the like and sent them home to the young wife whom he had left behind in the country.

Shirakawa's promise to take Suga to the theater had not been empty, and almost every night the faces of the Shirakawa family—Shirakawa himself with Tomo, Etsuko, Suga and two or three maids—were to be seen in the best seats at Fukushima's one and only theater, the Chitose-za.

In her newly made summer kimono of spotted crimson with tucks at the shoulders, Suga cut such a striking figure in the theater that even the actors in the green room commented on her to each other: "They say that's the new wife who's recently come to live with the chief secretary of the prefecture. The kind of face you might see in the picture on a young girl's battledore, isn't it?"

To the active members of the Liberal Party who so often had their secret gatherings raided and their leading figures arrested and who hated Shirakawa as their principal foe, the very sight of Suga was like a red rag to a bull. "He's the kind of man who deserves to be called a blight on the state—depriving the people of their rights while he lets tarts like that live in the lap of luxury." Neither Suga nor Etsuko, of course, had any idea that they were being watched with eyes darting hatred. Even Tomo always accepted more or less without question what she had been told by her husband and the wife of the governor: that those who defied the officials governing the nation in accordance with the Emperor's command, and who tried to stir up the people with talk of liberty and civil rights, were rogues who deserved punishment in the same way as arsonists and robbers. Toward the Emperor and the authorities she showed the same vaguely submissive attitude as to the feminine ethic that had taught her to yield to her husband's wishes in every respect, however unreasonable they might seem. Born in a country district of Kyushu near the end of the feudal period and barely able to read and write, she had no shield to defend herself other than the existing moral code.

The play at the theater was different every evening. One evening as they entered the box where the family always sat, Etsuko began to cry and complain that she was scared. The play was *Yotsuya Kaidan*, which was a great favorite among horror-loving patrons and often appeared on summer programs.

"It's all right, Miss. We'll shut our eyes together when the ghost appears," said Suga, who despite her usual timidity seemed relatively hard to scare and was watching the proceedings eagerly as she sat close by Etsuko's side. At bottom, Tomo thought, she's no weak woman.

The prologue gave way to the scene in the grounds of the temple of Kannon at Asakusa, then to the scene in which the heroine's father is killed, and by the time they had reached the scene in which Iemon's servant combs Oiwa's hair for her and it starts to fall out, Tomo's attention was entirely caught by the play and her eyes were riveted on the stage without so much as a sidelong glance at the others sitting by her.

On the stage, seated before a faded yellowish-green mosquito net, Oiwa was nursing her baby, her face wasted in childbirth yet beautiful still. Bitterly she lamented her fate—her damaged health and the husband who had suddenly turned against her following the birth of the baby; in vain she longed while still alive to see her younger sister and give her the comb that her mother had left them. The husband, Iemon, who had been lured away by the girl next door, wished to get rid of Oiwa. Telling her that it would

43

help her recover from the effects of childbirth, the girl's family had given her a poison intended to ruin her looks and thereby ensure that Iemon did not have regrets at leaving her, and the unsuspecting Oiwa, not realizing the deception, had taken the medicine repeatedly with every sign of gratitude.

Tomo watched the scene with a choking sense of pain; time and again she shut her eyes tightly in an effort to overcome the emotions that welled up irresistibly within her. Oiwa's fate, her uncomplicated trust in others, and her utter betrayal were all too familiar. Almost overinsistently, it seemed to Tomo, the play dwelt on the inevitable process whereby the love of a man and woman reached a peak of intensity only to cool off steadily into a kind of frozen hell. It was all too easy and too convincing to draw a parallel between Oume, who stole Iemon away, and Suga; between the cold but attractive Iemon and Shirakawa; between Oiwa, whose resentment at her cruel betrayal finally transformed her into a monstrous spirit of revenge, and herself. She watched as though spellbound those grotesque scenes in which the ghost of Oiwa took its powerful and protracted revenge. Etsuko, who at first had cried in terror and put her small hands half-jokingly over her face, had finally gone to sleep with her head pressed into Suga's lap, and was still limp and heavy as Tomo lifted her into the rickshaw that came to take them home.

The cool breeze of a summer evening blew in through the flap of the rickshaw. Tomo's eyes seemed to bore into Etsuko's face with its small, regular, doll-like features as the girl slept innocently with her tiny bun of hair pressed against Tomo's lap. Etsuko's older brother Michimasa, who was living at the home of Tomo's parents in the country, also came vividly to her mind. She must not become like Oiwa. Even though a madness many times the strength of Oiwa's sought to possess her, she would hug Etsuko to her all the more fiercely as though the act were a prayer. For if she were to became mad, what would happen to the children?

Although for Seki's sake she had seemed to accept the inevitable with such good grace, Tomo still put out her husband's bed every night in her own room in case it should be needed. She got out the quilts herself after the maids had retired for the night, and put them away again early in the morning. Every night the bed lay unclaimed, well-ordered and chill beside Tomo's.

One night Shirakawa, coming home unusually late, did not go to the new wing but came into Tomo's room.

"Send the women to bed . . . and bring some saké." His eyes were bloodshot and a blue vein pulsed at his temple. It was unusual for Shirakawa, who disliked saké, to order it at this hour.

"Tomo," he said, rolling up his sleeve for her to see. The upper half of his left arm was bound with a white bandage through which blood was seeping. Tomo went rigid, the bottle of warmed saké she had just brought still poised in her hand.

"Why! Where did you . . . ?"

"We raided a secret meeting of the Liberal Party. We arrested about ten of them, but the rest set on us as we were coming home." He laughed. "Lucky it was the left arm." His voice was high-pitched with tension and when he smiled his cheeks were stiff and tense. The opponents had been in earnest. He was lucky to have got home alive. The hand in which Tomo held the saké bottle trembled with the realization that it was to her he had come and not to Suga.

"It was lucky you weren't . . ." She faltered then stopped, staring at Shirakawa with startled eyes. His gaze flashed with a fierce light, he drained his saké cup at a gulp, then, sweeping her towards him with his arm, he crushed her against his chest. Her hair fell loose. With her face still pressed to his chest she lost her balance, clutched momentarily at the air in vain and collapsed

45

heavily against him. The saké from the bottle in her hand spilt over his chest and a smell of fermented liquor enveloped them as he tilted up her face and pressed his lips savagely to hers.

Shirakawa went back to the new wing at dawn. He had said not a word to Tomo about Suga, yet as she went back to bed alone it occurred to Tomo that he must have feared letting the young and still untouched Suga know the full force of his blood-smeared animality. And the knowledge that she had betrayed a certain passion with the husband who had rushed to her when he was wounded only heightened the hatred she felt for him, heightened it to the point where she could have clawed to shreds the face that seemed to sneer its perception of her foolishness.

The newspapers the next day reported that Chief Secretary Shirakawa had been returning from a raid on a secret meeting of the Liberal Party when he had been fired at by a number of its adherents; though slightly wounded himself, he had fired at one of his assailants with a pistol and killed him. Shirakawa had not told Tomo that he had fired his pistol, but the clearer it became that his coming to her after so many months had been but a way of giving vent to the murderous mental and physical excitement aroused by having killed a man, the more wretched Tomo felt.

The prefectural office and the whole town talked of nothing else for some time after, and Tomo could not fail to note that Suga's eyes when she was spoke of it to Etsuko showed not so much fear as a childlike admiration.

"I really think the master was wonderful," she said out on the veranda as their pretty hands moved together deftly weaving a cat's cradle of red cord.

"Why, Suga?"

"Well look at the danger he'd been through the other evening, and he didn't say a word. The next morning I saw him washing his face in a funny way, using only one hand to dip his towel in the water. I asked him what he'd done, but he just smiled and said the muscle in his arm was stiff. He didn't say anything at all about his injury."

"Do you think it didn't hurt, then?"

"I'm sure it did. I put a new bandage on for him this morning, and the wound was this big." Wrinkling her clearly marked eyebrows she shortened the string between her fingers to about two inches in order to show Etsuko. Etsuko merely thought that such a big wound must have hurt a lot, and was glad that her father had not been killed. But Suga, it seemed, was not content with this.

"They say that a real man doesn't show it when something hurts or worries him. The master kept it all to himself without a murmur. I think he's wonderful."

Working at her sewing in her own room, Tomo listened with chagrin to the note of innocent admiration in the words that the normally untalkative Suga used with such emphasis. In Suga's dreamy gaze and the gentle curves of her body there remained none of the unnatural stiffness that they had had when she first arrived; in the easy girlishness that pervaded them now, she was little different from Etsuko herself. It had taken Shirakawa a good month to relax her to the point where she was as open and vulnerable as this. But he had nearly reached his goal. Already vaguely disposed to cling to a man who petted and spoiled her like a father, Suga had now discovered a new and more heroic Shirakawa and was yielding to the pleasure of the discovery as mist gives way to sunlight. The first flower of love had begun to grow within her. Just as the fresh green orb of the tightly folded peony bud is seen one morning to be tinged with a flush of scarlet, so Suga too had begun to change her hue, and the change disturbed Tomo deeply. Nevertheless, there was no physical relationship so far. Something emanating from a woman who had known Shira-

47

kawa physically always affected Tomo with a sense of uneasiness. In Suga's case no such emanation had made itself felt so far.

Wondering just when and how Suga would give herself to Shirakawa, Tomo found herself even less able to sleep since Shirakawa had come to her room. Sometimes she could bear it no longer and getting up would push back the shutters, taking care not to disturb the sleeping Etsuko. Moonlight drifted across the grass in the garden wet with autumn dew, and the round window of the new wing flickered vaguely with the light of a lamp whose wick was turned low. In her mind's eye she could see how the light now shone on the yellow silk bedding, picking out the round shoulders of Suga's night kimono of purple striped silk as she lay peacefully sleeping; suddenly it seemed to Tomo that she herself was a great snake rearing its hooded head out of the light to stare at him and Suga, and hardly aware of what she did she clasped her arms tightly across her breast, shut her eyes tightly, and moved her lips as though crying out with her last breath, "Help me! Oh help me!" Many times she dreamed that she was on a ship tossed in a violent storm, rolling about inside its hull, unable to breathe.

One morning, Suga stayed in bed in her room, saying she had a headache. When Etsuko came back from school and went into the anteroom of the new wing carrying colored paper for making *origami*, Suga exclaimed "Miss Etsuko!" looking up from her pillow with eyes that were pleased at the familiar face but whose lids were swollen and puffy.

"Suga—what's happened to your eyelids?"

Etsuko spoke with no special significance but Suga blushed and pressed a hand to her eyes as though dazzled by the light. She felt as if Etsuko had peered in on the unforeseen events of the previous night. She harbored no resentment towards Shirakawa; in fact, lately she had begun to sense in him an indulgence, an inexhaustible dependability, for which she had hungered ever since leaving her father and mother. But her astonishment and shame remained; Suga had no feeling of any physical or mental flowering, only a kind of inner wilting with a sorrowful sense of something damaged, something destroyed. She hated even her parents, who had surely meant this when they told her never to go against her master's wishes. Something indefinable in her appearance began to betray the painful awareness that her body had been sold for money.

As Suga looked up with eyes full of melancholy, Etsuko's pale, oval face, so like Shirakawa's, seemed so fresh and fair that it might almost have soared away into the sky at any moment; she felt a vague enmity, too, but it was too ill-defined for Suga herself to distinguish it as such. At Etsuko's insistence she made all kinds of figures for her by folding the varicolored papers, all the while remembering with sadness, as though from a distant past, the innocent girl who only yesterday had been content to engage with Etsuko in artless pastimes such as these.

Once he had truly taken possession of her, Shirakawa's infatuation for Suga began to assume the proportions of an obsession. There was little he did not know concerning the other sex, whether geishas or ordinary women, but the fatherly affection that he felt for this unspoiled girl so far removed in age from himself rejuvenated him as though he had married again, and bathed his days in a glow of contentment. On a holiday, he went with Suga to the hot springs at Iizaka, taking with him his immediate subordinates and the proprietress of a restaurant he frequented. Here, Suga found herself addressed as "the mistress" and free to express herself to Shirakawa without constraint, so that each time she returned from a visit to the hot springs her beauty, like a great peony unfolding its many petals, seemed to grow a little more full-blown and voluptuous until finally she was no longer recognizable as the

49

maid of earlier days, remarkable for the charming timidity.

As his infatuation for Suga developed, Shirakawa no longer even set foot in Tomo's room, nor finally could Tomo herself bear any more the uncertainty of putting out her husband's quilts and waiting unheeded and alone.

It was generally held that Shirakawa had dissipated too much of his strength in pleasure to have any children other than Michimasa and Etsuko, yet even the remote possibility that Suga might have a child made Tomo shudder. Between husband and wife there yawned a gulf deeper than anything foreseen in the imaginings and silent surrenders so often repeated before she had brought Suga home with her. She must resign herself to the fact that henceforth the gulf would become deeper and wider each day, each night that passed. Only now did she realize with a sense of guilt the true reason why, in the inn at Utsunomiya on her return from Tokyo, she had been unable to talk frankly to her husband about the money he had entrusted to her. By nature incapable of being less than honest with others whoever they might be, she had never concealed anything from her husband where money matters were concerned. She had always despised as something shameful the traditional wife's savings made without her husband's knowledge, and the idea that she herself had now descended to the same level saddened her and at the same time gave her a new sense of resilience, as though her body had been reinforced throughout with fine wire.

Objectively speaking, there were any number of prominent and distinguished men in society today who had cast off their wives of many years like worn-out slippers and sent them back to their homes in the country, taking as their recognized spouses attractive women risen from the ranks of apprentice geishas or geishas. Since Tomo's straightforwardness and robust decency

50

had earned her the confidence of Governor Kawashima and his wife it seemed unlikely that even Shirakawa would do anything so outrageous, yet such was his infatuation for Suga these days that there was no knowing what scheme he might be hatching to drive her out. Before the Meiji Restoration, the family code had drawn a dividing line between wife and concubine that was not easily crossed, but now that the lesser retainers of remote country clans had come overnight to reign in the halls of power, the idea of the geisha house as a kind of antechamber to those halls had taken hold among men who aspired to high office, and the position of the wife, which inevitably depended on her husband's skill in public affairs, had become as vulnerable as a fragile, clinging vine.

Sometimes when her husband had seemed indecently blatant in his displays of affection for Suga, too careless of what others thought, Tomo even considered taking Etsuko and the money and going back to her home in far-off Kyushu. Yet each time her resolve was weakened by the thought of the future awaiting her daughter, now growing into such a beautiful young woman. Etsuko, fortunately, was on good terms with Suga and was loved by her father. If only Tomo herself could bear it, Etsuko would certainly be happier growing up in comfort as the daughter of a man of rank than in poverty in a remote country district of Kyushu.

This was the conclusion to which Tomo's better judgment always led her despite all her wilder impulses. It would be better for Shirakawa, too. However able he might be in his work it would only need the loss of his strictly upright, uncalculatingly honest wife for him sooner or later to make some fatal blunder in his official capacity also. Tomo, who knew that his difficult disposition had made him many enemies, had come almost without realizing it to see his nature at a step removed. In this she had already ceased to be the wife who obeyed her husband with implicit faith in his judgment, and was gradually acquiring the ability to view him dispassionately, as another human being. Innocent of learning, she had never been taught how to understand a person intellectually and was constitutionally incapable of letting her actions follow the natural dictates of her instincts. Only this had made it possible for her to live in unswerving allegiance to the feudal code of feminine morality and to take as her ideal the chaste wife who grudged no sacrifice for her husband and family. But now an unmistakable mistrust in the code that had been her unquestioned creed was making itself felt within.

Every day, every night, she came face to face in the same house with the woman who might dislodge her from her position as wife, talking to her as though it were the most normal thing in the world. How could she believe that such a life was decent and correct? How could she respect or love the husband who in his conceit and self-indulgence saw nothing more in the self-sacrifice and burning passion of over a dozen years than the loyalty of a faithful servant? Such a husband was no object for her love, such a life no more than an ugly mockery. She stood on in desperation in this sterile wasteland, firmly clasping Etsuko's tiny body to her, while she was mercilessly robbed of the husband she was to have served and the household whose mainstay she was to have been. She knew that to fall would mean never to rise again. The three-layered kimono with its family crests, the smooth servility of others, no longer helped her to live. She might have preferred, if she could, to shut her eyes to the present and return to the self that had trusted in Shirakawa's love, undismayed in the face of countless betrayals; but a force that flowed unceasingly like a raging stream carried her on despite everything, allowing her only to gaze back with many a deep sigh to the land left far upstream.

To her household Tomo presented a more energetic front than

ever; constantly she was on her guard never to show so much as a hair out of place. Far from fading into the background because of Shirakawa's infatuation for Suga, she seemed to counter Suga's growing beauty with such a sense of authority in her back and shoulders as she sat motionless in her room that even the maids and menservants who knew her so well would sometimes note it with a sense of surprise. Something forbidding emanated from her as she sat there without speaking, something that spurned all lies and deception and inspired more fear than did Shirakawa himself.

A letter in an untrained hand came for Tomo from her mother in the country. Though Tomo had told her nothing, a relative who had been staying at the home of someone who worked in the prefectural office and was connected with Shirakawa had spread the seeds of rumor on his return to Kyushu. Anguished at the thought of how Tomo must feel in the same house with a young concubine, her mother had laboriously spelled out the letter in her clumsy hand.

None of the other husbands in their family, she said, had got on in the world as Shirakawa had done, and Tomo should be grateful for her good fortune. It often happened that a man of ability took a concubine; at such times the wife should keep an even closer watch on herself so as not to lose her husband's love. His behavior was perhaps indiscreet in a man who had two young children, but she must not let jealousy upset her judgment to the point of bringing harm on herself, much less on her children. For all its illegibility and its uneven characters traced in an ink that now ran dry in mid-stroke, now blotted the paper, the letter betrayed the painstaking care of a mother attempting to convey to her child the emotion in her heart. Tomo, as she read, seemed almost to hear her old mother talking to her, coaxing her as when she was a child, and the tears flowed freely—self-indulgent tears

53

of a kind long forgotten, tears that by their very unfamiliarity brought home to her afresh the grimness of her present life. If feeling were set aside, her mother's injunctions were one and all no more than the tattered remnants of an outdated code that Tomo had already seen through and been forced to cast aside. The only part of her mother's letter that had any new message for Tomo's heart was contained in the last four or five lines:

For this fleeting world is a hell of evil, full of suffering, where man's shallow knowledge avails him nought and unawares he heaps sin on sin. Trust only, therefore, in the vow of the Lord Amida, morning and night forget not to invoke His name, and leave all else to Him . . . I should like to see you and talk to you more about the faith before I die. I hope sometime, if Yukitomo will give his permission, that you will come home.

As she read the passage, a vivid memory came of her mother reciting the invocation to Amida each morning, bowing deeply before their family shrine in Tomo's long-forgotten home in the country. Clinging to her mother's knees the infant Tomo had gazed up into her face, watching the lips that moved not as when they spoke normally but with a mechanical mouthing as they repeated incessantly the *Namu Amida Butsu*. Tomo too had chanted "*Namu Amida Butsu*" in imitation of her, but many years had lapsed since the words had passed her lips. All talk of the Buddha and of Amida had come to seem like a pack of lies to deceive children. The injunction in her mother's letter to leave everything to the Buddha only irritated her: what was she supposed to leave to him, and how? If there were some noble being, some god or Buddha, who could see all that went on in the human world, why did he not make life more decent for one who tried as hard as she to live truthfully? But despite these thoughts Tomo resolved that as soon as the opportunity arose she would at least arrange to go home as her mother wished. Whatever happened, she must hear directly from her mother those last wishes that could not be conveyed by letter alone.

The following spring, Governor Kawashima was appointed to a new post as Superintendent-General of the Metropolitan Police, and Yukitomo Shirakawa and his family followed him to Tokyo where they were installed with due ceremony in an official Police Department residence in the Soto-Kanda district of the capital. Tomo, who had had a copy of the family entry in the official register made in connection with Etsuko's change of school, was holding the flimsy piece of paper in her hand when she glanced down casually at it and a small cry escaped her. Directly after Etsuko's name was listed the name of Suga, as the adopted daughter of Yukitomo Shirakawa and of his wife Tomo.

The Handmaid

It was a typically bright, faintly chilly afternoon in the chrysanthemum season.

Kin Kusumi was trotting through the gateway of what was now the Imperial Palace carrying a basket of crackers that she had bought as a present on a visit to the temple of Kannon. She was on her way to the residence of Superintendent Shirakawa within the grounds, and since she had other business there today besides the usual polite inquiries after the family's health she was much preoccupied with the chances of success for her mission.

Newly built the previous year, Shirakawa's official residence was rumored to be second in size only to the Superintendent-General's own. A shapely pine tree grew in the center of the drive where the carriages swung round before the entrance, and beyond it was visible a spacious entrance hall with two rickshaws displaying family crests in gold drawn up before it. It seemed that someone was just going out. If it should be Mrs. Shirakawa, thought Kin, it would suit her purposes very well.

In theory long acquaintance had put their relationship on an easy footing yet still Kin found herself somehow constrained in Tomo's presence, her body growing tense as though she were under some pressure. The fact that today she had come from Suga's mother bearing a private message to the girl whom three years previously she had helped to place in the Shirakawa household made the thought of Tomo sitting there in her room still more disturbing.

The attractive girl in the elaborate hairstyle who emerged from within when Kin announced her presence at the side entrance— a maid, it seemed, though she was unknown to Kin—kneeled and bowed in the most formal manner, which flurried Kin so much that she had her summon Seki the housekeeper with whom she was more familiar.

"The mistress and the young lady are just going to a charity bazaar, and a foreign dressmaker is here getting them ready," Seki said. "Why don't you come in and watch?"

Her taste for the unusual aroused, Kin accepted the invitation and hurried in Seki's wake down a long corridor with a highly polished floor.

"That's a very pretty, graceful young maid you've got. When did she . . . ?"

"The month before last," said Seki, turning round and giving Kin a meaningful look. "The story before she came was that she was the very image of the Kabuki actor Eizaburo."

Kin nodded two or three times noncomittally, reflecting to herself that Suga's mother might be justified in worrying about the rumor that she had got wind of almost before anyone else.

"How old is she? And where does she come from?" The tone was casual, but Kin was aware that her voice as she pressed for more details sounded too strained for someone of her age, and that her neck was flushing hot below her ears.

"Sixteen, apparently. She's two years younger than Suga, but her height makes her look more or less the same, you know. It seems her father was in the service of the lord of the Toda clan. She has quite an opinion of herself, if you ask me."

"Well!" said Kin, drawing herself up exaggeratedly as a mark of her astonishment. "Even so, I suppose . . . she's still . . . just a . . . ?" She opened her eyes wider after each phrase, and Seki nodded in time with them.

"Not yet . . . no, so far . . . but sooner or later . . ." At this point she suddenly put a hand on Kin's skinny shoulder almost as though pouncing, and breathed hotly in her ear, "Then does the mistress know all about it then?"

"I suppose so . . . But listen—she's clapping for you."

Shoulders and hips swaying exaggeratedly as she went, Seki set off running with great strides along the corridor in the direction of the call.

At the entrance to the big room, in a Western dress embroidered with a fine pattern in yellowish brown and flared out below the waist by means of a whalebone corset, stood Tomo. Her old-fashioned face with its smooth, slightly sallow skin and its heavy eyelids emerged uncomfortably from the confines of the high, tight collar, which with her rather full, firmly compressed lips gave her in Kin's eyes the look of a Chinese woman. Tomo's gaze was directed to where her daughter Etsuko stood in front of a fringed, Western-style mirror in the center of the room, being helped into a Western-style dress by an English seamstress. Kin went and sat next to Suga, who kneeled at Etsuko's side, and watched in fascination.

Tall for thirteen though she was, Etsuko seemed like a small fawn as she stood beside the flaxen-haired seamstress with her long, giraffe-like neck. The heavily pleated velvet dress in lapis lazuli with heavy touches of indigo suited her face with its aquiline nose, cheeks of palest pink, and the crimson splash of the lips, giving her the unaccustomed dignity of some young woman of noble birth.

"The young lady's quite the little princess. So pretty," said the seamstress with a beaming smile as she finished the fitting, placing her hands on Etsuko's shoulders and turning her round for Tomo to see. Satisfaction seemed to gleam momentarily in

Tomo's eyes too, but her mouth did not soften. Etsuko, who seemed tense beneath Tomo's gaze, stood fidgeting, with frequent side-glances into the mirror.

"There's a Red Cross charity bazaar today, and the Super-intendent-General's wife said she wanted Etsuko to sell at a stall. I must say, I feel awkward got up like this, but . . ."

Tomo clearly disliked the whole business but was making the best of things. To strut to and fro in the Rokumeikan in the company of wives of distinguished persons was too ostentatious for a woman of Tomo's disposition, but the feeling that this was another of the duties of a high official's wife checked any desire in her to absent herself.

"The Empress is going to be there," put in Suga as she folded up the kimono that Etsuko had discarded. "And our young lady has the job of serving her tea."

"Well!" exclaimed Kin. "Be sure you're on your best behavior, Etsuko. I'm sure they've chosen you because you're so charming."

"Nothing of the kind," said Tomo. "Well, we must be going now. But we'll be back before dark, so take your time, Kin." And with Etsuko following, lifting the sides of her long skirt as she went, she set off walking toward the entrance hall.

After she had seen off the rickshaws bearing mother and child in their unfamiliar Western dress, Kin talked for a while with Seki in the hall, then went into Suga's room.

Suga's was a small room facing the back garden where pale pink sasanqua flowers were in bloom. With a band of rosy pink spotted silk over her triple bun, Suga was busily sewing a lined sash of Yūzen silk on the stitching stand, with a red needle holder resting on her lap. Seeing Kin, she laid aside her needle as though she had been expecting the visit and drew up a cushion by the side of the brazier for her.

"Have you seen my mother since you last came? I haven't heard from her lately."

Her home in Kokuchō was a mere stone's throw from the Shirakawa's official residence, but a girl in Suga's position could not come and go as she pleased. Whatever she might feel privately, Suga was officially registered as the Shirakawas' daughter, which meant that where society was concerned she had severed all connections with her own family. Although, having gained possession of Suga, Shirakawa lavished affection and advice on this girl young enough to be his daughter in such a way as to convince her that he was a paragon among men, all the while behind the scenes his cruel nature made him careful to tie her down with official restraints lest she run away. Used as she was to Shirakawa's affection Suga had no understanding of such forbidding aspects of the masculine mind, yet the realization that the mere mention of her parents or brothers and sisters would put Shirakawa into a vaguely bad temper made her too nervous ever to speak of them. Apart from the seasons of the Bon Festival and the New Year, when her mother came to offer greetings to the Shirakawas, her normal means of obtaining news of her own family was through Kin, who had first arranged for her to go into service.

"She came at the end of last month. She'd been to the temple at Hashiba, she said . . . She was very well. She said the beriberi in her legs has been much better this year, even since autumn set in."

"What about the shop? I heard something about them changing the type of business they do . . ."

"Oh that—it's hardly what you could call a change of business. It's just that besides bamboo skin they're going to take bamboo boxes and the like from the wholesalers."

"I wonder if they know what they're doing?" said Suga in a worried tone. "My brother's so good-natured he's always being

60

taken advantage of." When the eyelids that shaded her gem-like eyes opened and she gazed before her with moist, jet-black eyes her whole body seemed to be suffused with the somber pathos of a beautiful cat.

"They're all right," said Kin who disliked intensity and wanted to remove herself as quickly as possible from the shadows. "You don't have to worry." She waved a hand airily and, taking out a slender pipe from the tobacco case that hung from her sash, lit herself a pipeful of tobacco.

"What I really wanted to say, though, was that your mother was asking after you, Suga. She was worried about you."

"About me? I wonder why?" Her eyes blurred and she shook her head as though puzzled. For all her adult air there was still something childishly innocent in her face as she struggled to divine her mother's feelings.

"Well, I never! Here's your mother fretting herself, miles away from everything, and you on the spot not turning a hair."

At the time of her visit to Kin's house Suga's mother had really looked sick with worry. She had apparently thought of going to the Shirakawas' residence and inquiring directly of the mistress, but since that seemed rather tactless she had had the idea of asking Mrs. Kusumi to inquire indirectly how things really stood; and she started to relate her business with an expression so serious that from time to time she even forgot the ingratiating little smile that Kin had never before seen her without.

It had apparently begun with something said by the foreman of the men who tended the Shirakawas' garden. According to him, two maids from Honjo had come to the Shirakawas' for an interview that September. They were cousins, it seemed, and the interview had been arranged by a couple called Sonoda who came from the same district of Kyushu as the Shirakawas and were now in the antique business. One of the girls, whom the wife had brought in response to a direct request from Shirakawa for a good-looking maid, had stayed on in the house, while the other had gone home again.

According to what the maids had told the gardener, there were three maids living in at present, while it was Miss Suga who attended to the master's personal needs. When he gave parties or otherwise entertained at home, geishas and waitresses were summoned from the Shimbashi and Yanagibashi districts to wait on the guests, and there was no real need to bring in yet another maid. The mistress, being a long-suffering woman, kept everything to herself of course, and Etsuko was only too glad to have someone else to play with, but it was most unlikely that the girl would remain simply a maid. Almost certainly she would be seduced and installed before long as a concubine. Granted all this, what could Miss Suga be feeling about it? From the mistress' point of view, with Suga in the house it made little difference whether there was one concubine or two. But if the master was getting tired of Suga and thinking of installing a new girl in her place, how much longer would Suga be permitted to live a life of ease as though she were a daughter of the house?

After all, the master was fond of women—even though promotion had in fact taken him no farther than a reasonably influential position in the Metropolitan Police Agency, was he not used to summoning geishas from the best houses in Shimbashi like some younger member of the aristocracy?—and he could probably twist an unsophisticated girl like Suga around his little finger with no trouble at all.

Timid and näively trusting though she was, Suga's mother could not help bridling at the malice that lurked in the latter part of this report. She felt an intense anguish at this further proof of the envious slander directed at Suga from behind the scenes.

Suga might be negative and lacking in vitality in some ways, but, even as a child, she could never have been called stupid; she was a straightforward, unspoiled, tradesman's daughter who loved her mother and was quick to learn at dancing school. If only her parents had managed their affairs properly, who could tell what an advantageous match she might have made? To have put her into service with the Shirakawas in Fukushima in the summer of her fifteenth year, before she was even a real woman, was the act of a mother so heartless as hardly to deserve the name. Nevertheless, Suga seemed to feel sorry for the wretched parent thus obliged to sell her daughter, and though she never came to the house herself, she was sufficiently mindful of her family to send them, via others, presents of money and things to eat.

After they moved to the capital in the wake of Governor Kawashima, newly promoted to Superintendent-General of the Metropolitan Police, Shirakawa had become an important official at the Metropolitan Police Agency and was rumored to be living in high style on the taxes privately collected from the Yoshiwara gay quarters. Suga's mother would flush with gratification at stories that showed Suga cherished as a daughter in the home of this government official now at the height of his influence, but tales such as that brought by the gardener would set her anxiously listing to herself the family members other than Shirakawa. His wife, his daughter, the maids, the houseboy—suddenly she would see them all as hostile to Suga, and would long to fold in her arms the daughter thus trapped amid the thorns.

Whatever would happen to Suga if a new concubine came and the master's affections were diverted to her? At the time when she had first plunged her only daughter into such a situation, the mother had turned to Tomo as her only hope, beseeching her before she took her away to take a personal interest in the girl's welfare.

"If it should ever happen that the master's affections strayed and he got tired of her ... The very thought of what would happen to her keeps me awake at night."

As she sat listening, so correct with her hands clasped in her lap and not a seam of her kimono out of place, Tomo felt a profound sympathy for this woman whose very self-preoccupation and forgetfulness of all but her maternal love struck forcefully to her heart. It was all part of the strange role she had undertaken in coming, at her husband's command, to select a mistress for him that she should thus have encountered the devotion of a woman forced to sell her daughter and have thereby acquired another painful fetter on her heart.

"Try not to worry. However my husband's feelings may change I'll see to it that Suga doesn't go in need. How could I do otherwise when I'm taking home such a respectable girl? Come, now—you must have faith in me."

At this, the mother's last shreds of self-control had vanished and she had prostrated herself before Tomo. Hearing the clumsy, halting words with which she sobbed out her thanks, Tomo had had to fight back the bitter tears that came welling up.

Suga's mother remembered all this now. She felt an urgent desire to meet Tomo and have her confirm once more what she had said then, but when it came to the test she had lost her nerve and come to see Kin instead.

"You mean Miss Yumi, don't you?" said Suga when Kin had finished, blinking her eyes as though the light was too strong for them. "If that's it, then there's nothing worth speaking to the mistress about. Just tell Mother, please, that there's nothing to worry about."

"Really ...? No, I suppose there isn't." Kin rested the mouthpiece of her pipe against her cheek and nodded with an equivocal expression.

"Then, so far as you can tell there's no sign that the same thing's going to happen to Yumi?" Kin added.

"Oh no, I didn't mean that." An unintended smile appeared on the cheeks that were like cream-colored handmade paper. The smile was devastatingly innocent but Kin shivered as though an icy hand had brushed the back of her neck.

"It's already happened," Suga continued. "Before long the master will have settled things with her parents and she'll be coming to live with me in this room."

She spoke smilingly and without hesitation but Kin listened with rounded eyes, the mouthpiece of her pipe still resting forgotten against her cheek.

"I see . . . Then surely, your mother's justified in worrying, isn't she?"

"But there's nothing at all to worry about. Yumi's a straightforward girl, more like a boy in her outlook, so she and I seem to be well matched."

"That's all very nice, I suppose, but if the master should turn his affections to Miss Yumi it would be no laughing matter, you know."

"It's all right," she said with the same innocent smile as before. It was a smile without substance, as if she were being drawn uncomprehendingly down into some unknown darkness.

Again a creeping horror down Kin's back made her look at Suga intently. Suddenly she felt a surge of curiosity to peer behind the concealing curtain and discover just how Shirakawa was bending Suga to his purpose.

" 'All right'? You mean, the master talks about everything like that to you?"

"Well, not exactly everything . . ."

She broke off, her cheeks aflame, her expression embarrassed. She seemed ashamed at having said something she shouldn't.

65

"But, I mean to say, your mother's not going to be satisfied with your words alone. If you want to stop her worrying, you'll have to do it properly . . . I can see your mother will have to come and talk to the mistress."

"Oh, really!" Suga frowned and shrugged slightly as though in irritation. Just then a tortoiseshell kitten that had been curled up in a ball on a cushion of Yūzen silk came over to her with a tinkling of its bell, so Suga picked it up and put it on her lap. Stroking its soft fur she began talking slowly, without looking Kin in the eye, almost as though to herself.

"The master takes great care of me. He says I'm not as strong as most women and I shall die young if I overdo things . . . That's why that happened to Yumi. The master's used to geishas and courtesans, so he knows a lot about how women work. Right from the start, I've looked on myself almost as a daughter, so I've never felt jealous or anything. Perhaps it's the difference in our ages. But even the mistress doesn't know that, so you mustn't tell anybody."

As she finished speaking, Suga's face looked suddenly grown-up and her eyelids veiled her gaze. Without her realizing it, an immense vacancy had spread itself across her bewitching features, draining them mysteriously of all expression.

After Kin had left with the dissatisfied look still on her face, Suga sat for a while prey to some inexplicable sadness, rubbing the kitten's throat and gazing out with tear-filled eyes at the rabbit's-ear pink of the sasanqua blooms in the garden. Despite herself she felt ashamed that she should feel no jealousy toward her rival Yumi, when her mother and Kin were both so obviously distressed.

Although she had been reared in the plebeian districts of Tokyo, her parents had been decent people, and she knew nothing of relationships between men and women. At dancing lessons she had always taken the male role and, in her character as this or that popular romantic hero, was used to being clung to by the heroine; at such times the dancing teacher had often told her to put more "sensuality" into her dance, and sensual desire and love had become inseparably associated for her with the brilliant costumes of the dance and with the music for voice and samisen that accompanied it.

Even since her arrival in the Shirakawa household and her discovery of men's nature—a discovery made through her body and in the dark, far from bright colors and music—Suga had cherished in her heart, quite untouched by her direct relationship with Shirakawa, a shining world of enchantment where the heartrending strains of the old ballads came drifting in forlorn snatches, and the brilliant colors of trailing sleeves and skirts wove in and out with tantalizing deliberation. For some strange reason, this fantasy in no way negated the actuality of Shirakawa.

Shirakawa was a man who even in his own home sat aloof and rarely allowed himself to smile. When he drank, he was not one to lose his dignity on a mere two or three cups of saké. Nor was this solely a desire not to show himself at a disadvantage before Tomo, for at all times his air was chaste and aloof, as though he were quite indifferent to the other sex. He was more fastidious about his appearance than the average woman; often he would complain of this and that to the man who came from the draper's to see to their clothes, and the white socks he wore with Japanese dress had never been known to show a wrinkle.

When Suga got out his clothes and helped him on with them, or stood by him adjusting the mirror to a convenient angle as he shaved, or attended to any other of his personal needs, the cool neatness and youthfulness of his person gave a lift to Suga's spirits that made her body move with a lightness it never had when she waited upon the mistress. Yet if asked if this meant that she loved Shirakawa, she would still have been unable to reply. For all the appreciation that Shirakawa lavished on her person as though on some rare jewel, a sense of having being robbed, of being captive, still lay heavy in Suga's heart, so that her beauty, although she was not aware of it, was a shadowed beauty as of cherry blossoms on a cloudy day.

She stroked the kitten's small white belly, ruffled the fur on its back, felt its tiny claws scratching at her hand, and suddenly hugged it so tightly to her that it raised a plaintive wail.

"I'm the same as you, aren't I?" she sighed.

She knew that however a kitten might struggle it was no match for a human being. And intuitively she sensed the cruel, merciless soul that lay beneath Shirakawa's exterior polish and refinement.

Something had happened while they had still been in Fukushima.

Among the young subordinates of Shirakawa who frequented the house there was a shortish man called Kazabaya who, whenever he passed Suga in the corridor, would brush seemingly unawares against her shoulder or arm, or stare unblinkingly into her face. One day at a saké party at which Kazabaya was sitting at the foot of the table, some turn in the conversation led him to ask Suga to show him her ring of inlaid gold.

Thinking nothing of it, Suga took off and showed him the ring, which he promptly pocketed and refused to return despite all her entreaties. Afraid to talk too loudly in front of others she let the matter drop, beside herself with fear at the thought of what would happen if Shirakawa should find out after Kazabaya had gone.

She would never have mentioned the matter directly to Shirakawa, of course, yet before the night was out he had realized from the unusual shrinking of her immature body that something was wrong. Clasping her fingers that were stiff with cold one by one in the dark, he said casually, "Your ring's gone," and her smooth white skin suddenly turned to gooseflesh and she began to tremble like a frightened mole.

"Did you give it to somebody?" Gently, like a father, he stroked the skin on her back and arms, and she curled herself up against him and began to sob. Then in fits and starts, hiccuping between her sobs like a scolded child, she blurted out the story of how Kazabaya had taken the ring from her.

"Don't be silly. There's nothing to cry about . . . The young fellows often play that sort of joke. Even so, you'd better take care—that kind of thing can lead to the most dreadful trouble."

He put an arm around her as he spoke, while with the other hand he used the sleeve of his kimono to wipe away her tears and separated strand by strand the wet hairs that clung to her cheek.

Assuming that the affair had ended that evening, Suga was horrified a few days later to hear that on a visit to Higashiyama Spa with his colleagues from the prefectural office Kazabaya had been beaten up in a drunken quarrel and had broken his hipbone. Among those who had gone with him were several police officers who were at Shirakawa's beck and call. Ever after, when Suga saw Kazabaya come limping to Shirakawa to listen humbly to his behests, she felt a surging sense of pain. Nowadays, Kazabaya averted his eyes from her as though afraid to catch sight of even a lock of her hair.

The master was a man to be feared, she realized, a man who might do anything once his anger was aroused. From this time on, the image of Kazabaya limping along lurked somewhere in the back of her mind even when she and Shirakawa were at their most relaxed and intimate.

"I've sown too many wild oats to be a father again," Shirakawa would say sometimes, "but even if I hadn't, I'm sure with a body like yours you couldn't have a child."

69

The words branded themselves indelibly on her mind. She had no particular desire for a child by Shirakawa, yet to be dismissed as a woman who could not bear children shrouded her heart with the forlorn sensation of being on a journey through the dusk with no place to rest at the end of the road.

She was, after all, a servant, with no prospects in life. Her one consolation was that by doing this she could ensure that her mother and brother lived a little more comfortably. Even if she left, she would never again become the unspoiled girl she had once been, and with a wife already in the same household the addition of one more woman like herself made little difference. From the time when she came to feel that this might well happen, Suga began to feel almost a kind of identification with Yumi in her hairstyle, her boyish face, her swarthy complexion and her tall, clean-limbed look.

Shirakawa must have done something to Yumi, somewhere, for Suga found her one day standing by the heavy doors of the white-walled storehouse, her narrow shoulders shaking with sobs. "What's the matter? Yumi, tell me what's the matter," she said, resting a hand on Yumi's shoulder and peering round into her face. Yumi promptly hid her face in the sleeve of her kimono and wept. At each heave of her shoulders Suga felt a vague sensation in her own body that told her quite clearly, with no need to ask, the cause of Yumi's misery.

"There, Yumi . . . I know, I know. It was the same with me, after all . . ."

The tears came flooding into Suga's eyes as she spoke and her voice was thick with emotion. Yumi peered up at her as though hearing her voice for the first time, saw Suga's large, tear-filled eyes, and buried her head against Suga's breast in a violent fit of weeping as though what she saw had provoked a fresh wave of unhappiness. Weeping with her, Suga stroked Yumi's narrow shoulders; the body was strong and flexible like young bamboo, with a thin layer of firm flesh over a slight bone structure. The amber, somewhat coarse-textured skin too had a touch of masculinity that was agreeable to Suga.

"My mother and father will be cross . . . that this should happen to me . . . I'm so ashamed." She wept afresh between each phrase. Yet there was a certain resilience in Yumi's lamentations that had been lacking in Suga's own sorrow. Suga found it attractive. Suddenly, her heart was filled not with jealousy but with a wish to be close to Yumi, to put her arms around her so that they could share their common woe.

"Yumi, let's try to help each other. I'm not worth much, but won't you let me be your sister?"

"Will you really? Suga . . . I, I . . ." Heedless of her elaborate hairstyle, she buried her head in Suga's lap.

That evening Yumi came to Suga's room, where she talked to her of her upbringing and her family. They were poor; the only working member left was her elder sister's husband at the ward office, but at one time her father had been a bodyguard of a minor feudal lord and her mother had been in service at the lord's residence. At the urging of Mrs. Sonoda, Yumi had come to the Shirakawa household in the belief that she was going to learn polite manners, but the way things had turned out made her suspect that those responsible had secretly intended it from the time they first helped her to get the position. Shirakawa said that he would take responsibility for her as his adopted daughter in the same way as Suga, but she doubted whether her stubborn father would agree. It would be unbearably embarrassing for her if her father came complaining that his daughter had been ruined. The very idea, she told Suga with an expression of intense emotion, made her want to go away somewhere and hide herself.

Excitement and the tears that stained her cheeks had given Yumi's face, with its tightly knit eyebrows like those of a handsome boy, a still more simple beauty. The fact that her sorrow was untouched by bitterness at the wrong she had been done softened Suga's own heart and gave her a sense of kinship with the girl.

The bazaar that day had gone even better than expected, it seemed. At dusk, Tomo and Etsuko came home ahead of Shirakawa, who had come to the bazaar as a guest; they carried with them a bundle of cakes and cosmetic bags that he had bought as presents for those who had stayed at home.

Shedding her constricting Western dress and donning a kimono of heavy yellow silk with a loose jacket in Yūzen dyed silk, Etsuko came to Suga's room and told her everything she wanted to know about how she had served tea to Her Majesty the Empress.

"Yes . . . I think you could say she's pretty. You know—she's rather like our Yumi." Having let this slip, Etsuko shrank into herself and glanced behind her. If her mother had been there, she would certainly have been severely scolded for such a disrespectful comparison. So strict was Tomo's training that Etsuko always seemed more lively and childlike when she was with Suga or the maids. Suga herself felt a natural sympathy with the innocent way in which Etsuko would cling to her. Having had a mother who did up her hair for her, bought her pretty hair ornaments, and generally spoiled her, there were times when she felt something akin to pity for this child who though still small could never fully be herself with either parent and was always on her guard in a way that was unnatural in a child.

"Do you like Yumi, Etsuko?"

"Oh yes, very much!"

"More than me, I think?"

"Oh, *no*! You're more . . . but no, I like you both." She shook her head as if perplexed. Suga looked put out but was captivated at the same time by the openness and straightforwardness of the girl's nature; it was only when she was joking thus with Etsuko that she felt a clearing of the spirit as though she herself were a child once more.

That night, Tomo felt a chill run over her body when Suga brought the message for her to come to Yukitomo's bedroom. For all his good temper after the Rokumeikan bazaar when he had told her to go home ahead of him with the shopping they had done, he had been tense and ill-tempered on his return later that night. She was used to his moodiness, and she knew from long experience that at no time was he so out of sorts and difficult as when a clear, cold gaze was contradicted by a pulsing blue vein at his temple and when the joints of his fingers seemed stiff, his thumb crooked. And at such times it was his habit, rather than seeking to disperse his tension in Suga's company, to summon Tomo and question her in detail about the management of the family finances or the supervision of their assets. Tomo had no objection to his making an opportunity for them to talk together alone without the concubines, for at least once or twice every month there were decisions they had to make jointly, but she hated that at times when something had displeased him it should be she who received the full force of his resentment. Going into her husband's bedroom, where two sets of quilts were set out side by side, she felt like an accountant about to have his books inspected by his superior. The thought that today when he was particularly irascible she must necessarily bring up the matter of Yumi made her still more reluctant to enter the room where he was waiting.

Two or three days previously, Tomo had received a letter from

Yumi's father tastefully written in the Chihagi style of calligraphy. Respectful inquiries after their health soon gave way to a suggestion that the unforeseen change in her circumstances that had been thrust on Yumi was somehow half Tomo's own responsibility. Why had Shirakawa needed to violate Yumi when he had a wife and a mistress already? Though he was head of the household, to deprive a young woman of her virginity without her father's consent was going too far. Her virginity, either way, could never be recovered, so what steps did he propose to take? He would call on Shirakawa in the near future to hear his intentions in the matter. The phraseology was obsequious but the bullying tone was unmistakable.

Tomo also knew through Sonoda, however, that Yumi's father had been dimly aware and privately hoping that this would happen when he put her in service. That the father should send such a pompous letter when he almost certainly had an eye to the remittances that would make life easier if Yumi became a concubine like Suga was doubtless no more than a sign of the importance of pride to an old man of samurai stock, yet Tomo herself felt more sympathy with the unsophisticated straightforwardness of Suga's mother and with her frank appeal that carried no pretense of equality. The greed she sensed behind the lines of well-formed characters and the well-turned phrases was to her far the more base, and she stayed a while with the letter in her hand, a grim little smile playing about her mouth.

When she entered the bedroom, Shirakawa was in his nightwear, one elbow resting on the small mahogany writing table beside the lamp as he made corrections in red ink on some official documents.

"Why don't you change?" he said, directing an ill-tempered look at her. Quietly, she went out into the anteroom again. The sound of rustling fabric reached him with an odd clarity. She must be undoing her sash of stiff silk; he put down his writing brush and listened to the indications of slow, heavy motion that were melancholy and monotonous yet powerful as the waves on a wintry sea in their silent suggestion of the body and the voice so familiar to his sight and hearing after nearly twenty years of marriage. They summoned up forgotten scenes that came and went as she moved, scenes of the mountain streams of his home in Kyushu and the deep snows that buried the northeastern districts of Honshu where his work had taken him. Like a shadow that he could never leave behind, Tomo would gradually age in this house, growing more and more like a family ghost till finally she died. Vaguely he sensed the deep-seated, icy will so far removed from love or self-sacrifice that made her follow so submissively the vagaries of his will. It aroused in him some strong emotion akin to hatred. To him she was, quite unlike Suga or Yumi, something formidable, an enemy entrenched in a fortress that no assault could reduce. Yet today he was sick at heart and would gladly have put aside the stiffness in which he normally encased himself and talked to her easily and familiarly, as they had when they were young.

Why should that be? Today, he had seen a ghost in broad daylight.

Although he had accompanied Superintendent-General Kawashima to the ball that was held in the great drawing room of the Rokumeikan following the charity bazaar, he had no interest in Western music or dancing and had been sitting on a sofa in the antechamber quenching his thirst with white wine that a waiter had brought him.

Someone had tapped him on the shoulder. Turning casually, he had seen a man in a frock coat standing there, a man with a handlebar mustache and piercing eyes about whose bitter mouth there played a smile that was half aggressive and half placating.

"Hello, Shirakawa! I still have to thank you for all you did for me in Fukushima."

It was a young man called Hanashima, a follower of Unno Takachu, the political leader. At the period when Shirakawa, acting under orders from Governor Kawashima, had clamped down so fiercely on the civil rights movement in Fukushima, Unno had been bound fast and subjected to merciless interrogation, then tried in Tokyo and sent to jail where he was reported to have died of disease. Hanashima had apparently bragged that he could happily eat Shirakawa's flesh and still hunger for revenge. Now, the broken-down, disheveled man of those days had given way to a figure of neat elegance with abundant hair parted in the very center and an aura of cologne that suggested a recent return from the West. Shirakawa was understandably taken aback.

Hanashima threw out his chest and let out a peal of laughter, from sheer pleasure, it seemed, at having so startled the normally imperturbable Shirakawa.

"Don't look so surprised. I suppose you thought I was dead, didn't you? But come—how silly of you! What would the people do if I died while cunning officials like you were still at large? Look—you see this nightless city with its glittering chandeliers? Do you know what it is? It's the death throe of the clan government—the flaring-up of the candle before it flickers out! However much you struggle against it, the Constitution will be promulgated in another year or two. Then, like it or not, there'll be a National Assembly. The members will be chosen by the people, so there'll be no more of your officials appointed at the discretion of the government. Your reign will soon be over. Very soon you lackeys of bureaucracy will be done for. You'll see the rising strength of the masses—you men who use your authority only to grab after personal profit."

Hanashima went off roaring with laughter, leaving Shirakawa almost speechless for a while. This state of deflation was totally unlike his usual self. The small groups of people about him did not matter: they might well have taken them for close friends, so hearty had Hanashima's manner been. But what had happened to the Hanashima who as they took him under guard through the snow had cried out that he could not breathe because the ropes were too tight? In the ballroom, he could see the couples in their fine clothes, hands linked, like a stream of gay flowers as they glided to the strains of Western music over the parquet floor beneath the sparkling light of the gasoliers. Hanashima who had left him just now was already dancing happily, his arms about a beauty in an evening dress of purple satin that revealed her naked shoulders. The effect was to make Shirakawa feel oddly forlorn and isolated.

It was only four or five days previously that Superintendent-General Kawashima, a man not easily daunted, had said, his large heavy-lidded eyes creasing in a grim frown:

"If we don't get complete control within the next year or two, it's all up with us. Personally, I don't want to live to see that day come."

Could it be that the demon superintendent, the man who had devoted all his energies to suppressing the popular campaign for civil rights, had come to realize that the new age rolling towards them like the sea at full tide was something against which no resistance was possible? Shirakawa could not avoid a sense of disheartenment at the crack he saw appearing in the disposition of this obdurate man who had once so blithely seized people's homes in what amounted to daylight robbery, and pulled them down in order to make way for a prefectural road—the man who had happily tolerated the poisoning by mineral wastes of a whole area

77

along the banks of the Watarase river so that the copper mine at Ashio might prosper—all this done in the name of loyalty to the state.

Today he had caught sight of Taisuke Itagaki, president of the Liberal Party, which probably meant that Hanashima had come in his party. At the thought of a national assembly being convened and of Unno and Hanashima winning seats in it, whence to carry on their championship of civil rights, Shirakawa, like it or not, could not avoid a sense that the days when he and other bureaucrats had reigned unchallenged were slipping into the past. Little by little, he felt himself menaced by an end similar to that which had overtaken any number of trusted followers of powerful figures in the not so distant past.

He wanted to place his daunted spirit in Tomo's protective arms. The emotion he felt now was one that he could not possibly divulge to Suga or Yumi, whom he petted as one would care for a goldfish or a caged bird. The wound could only be soothed, the blood only staunched, by a woman stronger and more resilient of will than himself. And yet he was merely imposing a maternal image on one in whom the love once sensitive enough to have detected in him such a subtle injury of the soul had long since turned utterly to ashes. The sight of Shirakawa's ill-tempered face merely made Tomo fold her arms defensively and avoid anything that would aggravate his mood, much as she would have avoided touching an angry boil. The advent of a new concubine in addition to Suga merely made her apprehensive as to how Yumi's nature would develop in their household, and failed entirely to kindle any keen fires of jealousy.

So it was that when Tomo that night broached the subject of the letter from Yumi's home her voice was quiet, with a hesitant tone as though it were she who was making an unreasonable demand, as though she were on her guard lest by giving her husband offense she should complicate things still further.

"Since her family are former samurai, I'm afraid things are likely to be rather awkward."

"I doubt it. According to Sonoda, the girl called Mitsu who came with her was secretly worrying in case she became a concubine. It seems Yumi's mother worked as a maid on the private quarters of Lord Toda, so she should be well up in these things. I expect it all comes down to a question of the family's honor, and ultimately of money."

He spoke as though the affair had no direct connection with himself, resting a sharp gaze on Tomo as he spoke. He was irritated not so much by the affair of Yumi in itself as by the fact that Tomo seemed less perturbed than when she had first brought Suga home.

"How much?" asked Tomo, looking him in the eye. She too felt a sense of distaste at her own moral indifference, at the absence of offended sensibilities with which she had learned of the loss of Yumi's virginity.

"The same as in Suga's case, I imagine. If anything," he said coldly, with an air of finality, "it should be cheaper this time." The sneering implication was that Yumi was a less substantial, shallower kind of girl than Suga. For he had loved Suga besides Tomo, and Yumi besides Suga, and what difference had it made to the world in which he lived? He folded his arms with a sense of desolation, fighting against the loneliness that swept through him like a chill, dark wind.

2

The Moon of the Twenty-sixth Night

"The carriages are coming . . . The bride! The bride!"

The cry rang out in a stentorian voice from one of the workmen in traditional livery stationed at the gate as the men pulling the rickshaws came bravely running up the sloping drive between the shrubbery, and suddenly the entrance where they awaited the bride stirred like a flock of birds rising into the air.

The wet-nurse Maki who had been suckling the baby in the distant wing of the house roused herself at the distant sounds. Softly she withdrew the arm that served as a pillow for the now sleeping Takao's tiny head and drew her kimono together over her uncovered breast as she rose and went to the veranda. Although the baby normally never left her side, Tomo had today moved Takao together with Maki to the distant wing, lest the young bride whom one day he would learn to call Mother should be disturbed on the very night of her nuptials by an infant's cries.

Seen from the second story of this house built on a high, gently sloping stretch of land, the sea off Shinagawa that the eye by day could take in at a glance was veiled in the evening haze of high spring, a haze that turned the green of the garden's trees to a dark

81

blue and left only the full-blooming cherry trees looming like great, pale mauve parasols here and there on either side of the gently sloping drive. Just now the bride's rickshaw, preceded by that of the go-between, was winding its way beneath the umbrellas of blossom up the gentle slope. In the carriage, whose flap was drawn back, the bride sat with head deeply bowed. The elaborate hairstyle with the white bridal headdress surmounted by decorative combs and pins swayed heavily, and the scarlet of what must have been the long outer kimono with its embroidered figures stood out clearly in the gathering gloom. The light of the lanterns hanging on poles at the entrance or held in the hands of those waiting to receive her still failed to outshine the remaining daylight and glowed an apricot orange that gave a still more unearthly beauty to the bridal procession. Maki watched entranced, with a sense that she had seen it all in a dream, until a sudden thought occurred to her, the excitement shriveled, and the bride in all her finery seemed suddenly a figure of misfortune.

She must be coming with no suspicion as yet of the young master's true nature. Maki, whose own marriage had failed, felt sorry for her. Taken on as wet-nurse for Takao when puerperal fever had claimed his mother soon after his birth more than a year previously, even the placidly unquestioning Maki had by now more or less grasped the extraordinary complexity of the situation within the Shirakawa household.

Yukitomo Shirakawa had left government service shortly after the promulgation of the new Constitution. The sudden stroke that at the early age of fifty or so had taken the life of Superintendent-General Kawashima, whose friendship he had enjoyed for so many years, had been the direct cause of his retirement. There was in fact no one else among his superiors before whom the stubborn Yukitomo was prepared to bend his own will, nor had he, having succeeded during his years in office in accumulating more than ample wealth to take care of his old age, any mind to serve a second master. More than this, though, having himself been reared on the Confucian learning and martial skills considered appropriate in a lower-ranking samurai of the Hosokawa clan, he felt it beyond his ability to compete with the slowly mounting interest shown by the younger bureaucrats of the Meiji government in new knowledge brought back from the West, or with their insidious tendency to dabble in English and seek to implement Western-style legal theories.

It was unbearable to his old-fashioned pride that his subordinates should patronize him; and to stay in his present office without the backing of Kawashima might expose him to still direr ignominy. Worse still, if a national assembly were established and government by elected representatives came into force, it would follow that, sooner or later, political go-getters such as the Hanashima whom he had met at the Rokumeikan would come to the fore as representatives of the new regime. To avoid these perils that he saw ahead, Yukitomo had voluntarily withdrawn from official service. His purchase of a large house, once the residence of a foreigner, near Gotenyama in Shinagawa, was likewise aimed to give him a stronghold where he could live out his remaining years as he pleased with no one to impose on him. The mansion on its high eminence was his castle; it was also the burial mound of the ambitions that had been shattered in their prime.

Within his home, Shirakawa reigned as a despot, like the clan lords of the feudal age just past; neither his wife Tomo nor his concubines Suga and Yumi could have enjoyed a day's peace of mind in this house had they had not adapted themselves to his ostentatious, irascible temperament. Etsuko had been married the year before, to a bachelor of laws newly returned from studying in the West.

The only person in the household who could not fit in with Yukitomo was his son Michimasa.

Mishimasa, who had been born to the Shirakawas while they were still at their home in the country following an early marriage, had been brought up in the home of an aunt and uncle at Kumamoto in Kyushu while Yukitomo had been moving from one official post to another in northeastern Honshu. By the time they had finally settled in Tokyo and fetched him to live with them again, he must have been already fifteen or sixteen. Yukitomo had tried to educate him: had put him in an English academy, had sent him to the newly founded Tokyo College; but though Mishimasa had average powers of retention, his twisted disposition made it utterly impossible for him to strike up a close acquaintance with anybody. At academy and college alike, he was spurned by everyone with whom he might have made friends, so that in the end there was no alternative but to leave him to lead the life of a young recluse at home.

In the proud Yukitomo his warped offspring inspired not so much pity as an extreme antipathy. The contempt that such a lack of sympathetic qualities would have inspired in him even in a stranger became an unbearable sense of shame when its object was his own flesh and blood.

Even at home, he would not take his meals with Michimasa, who lived in the houseboy's room with a nephew from the country who was staying with them until he got married.

"A boy shouldn't be treated as a man until he's independent of his parents," Yukitomo said.

For Tomo, it was a double anguish. Suga and Yumi, half servant though they were, were living openly in the master's room with him, while the son and heir Michimasa lived in the houseboy's room with its *tatami* yellowed with age, where the sight of him sitting opposite their nephew Seizō, shoveling rice greedily into his mouth with chopsticks grasped clumsily in his fist, filled her with such despair that she wanted to cover her eyes. On the other hand, whenever Michimasa came into a room where Yukitomo was present, his father's eyes would take on a hard glint and dwell as though with unbearable loathing on Michimasa's clumsy, noisy movements and his face, which with its lumpish forehead and large nose was like one of the grotesque masks used in ancient court dances. Tomo, who at the best of times was forever on the lookout for any change in Yukitomo's mood, would become still more nervous when Michimasa was there, on tenterhooks lest he should say something stupid that would anger his father yet again.

If Michimasa had been a normal young man who happened to be rejected by his father, Tomo would naturally have covertly taken his side, and this in turn would have deepened the love between mother and son, but only too often Michimasa's speech and behavior were such that even his mother was seized by the same loathing as Yukitomo.

When Tomo considered that it was she herself who had given birth to Michimasa, that the father was unmistakably Yukitomo, it seemed absurd that Michimasa's heart should harbor no trace of love for any living creature other than himself, that he should be fated not to inspire love in any other person, and she quailed at the hopelessness of doing anything about that absurdity.

Why should they have had such a child? Could it be a punishment for having let him grow up away from them that he had turned into such a man?

When Tomo saw the sons of her relatives and acquaintances growing up into young men who, if not outstanding, were at least average, she would compare them with Michimasa and examine once more her own behavior in the past. But apart from the fact that she had let him spend his childhood years with his aunt and uncle in the country she could not believe that she, at least, had created any unfavorable circumstances such as might have fostered such a special nature in him. Unwilling to let the children be influenced by their father's self-indulgence, she had never once complained of him to Michimasa or Etsuko. The blame for the eternal immaturity of Michimasa's nature could only, in the long run, be attributed to the immaturity of her own body at fifteen when she had given birth to him. Conceived in a womb imperfectly matured, he had been born with a mind incapable of growth. Could any child, indeed, be more unfortunate?

In theory, however much everyone else shunned Michimasa, Yukitomo and Tomo, as his mother and father, should have enfolded him in a love given without stint. In fact, though, even his mother could not lavish affection on Michimasa as he wandered aimlessly through life like a lost child, apathetically, with a mind refusing to mature inside the body of a full-grown adult. The idea inspired Tomo with a violent distaste for the unwillingness to suffer fools gladly that was so stubbornly rooted within her own character.

At the very least, then, she wanted to find him a wife so that he could have children and lead a life like other men. Her secret wish had perhaps conveyed itself tacitly to Yukitomo, for a few years earlier Michimasa had finally taken his first wife—whereupon, partly from consideration of how things would look to the bride, he had at last come to be treated, on the surface at least, as the young master of the Shirakawa household.

These tales of the past Maki knew only by hearsay, from Seki and the other maids. At first she had tended to wonder at and despise a family that did not give its elder son his due, however wanting his character might be in some respects, but before long she too had changed her mind and begun to consider it natural that even his own parents should shun him. With the autocratic Yukitomo, the morally upright Tomo, and with Suga and Yumi—

for all their wilfulness, their straitlaced attitudes, their feminine secretiveness and changeability—she could, as she got used to them, find something in each to which she responded, but with Michimasa the longer she was with him the more she felt what a relief it would be if he were not there. Michimasa was close-fisted, gluttonous, and snappish with the servants. When food was put before him he would wolf it down like a starving child, and whenever he opened his mouth to speak he invariably inspired a sense of disgust as though he gave off some foul odor. His mere presence was enough to cast an ugly pall over those about him.

Even the affection that Yukitomo and Tomo showed for the infant Takao frequently roused his anger. He would look at Takao in Maki's arms with the air of an animal that shows no feelings of joy yet has limitless reserves of rage and jealousy, and would say maliciously, "God—what's the point of continually putting fresh clothes on a baby like that? What a waste!" And he would scowl into the baby's face with his vacant eyes aglint, as though he might start beating it at any moment. Every time this happened Maki had the uneasy feeling that she herself was included in his hatred, and would reflect that perhaps Takao's mother was better off dead after all. No woman, she was convinced, be she saint or vilest sinner, could be happy married to a man like that.

Miya, who had come today as bride, was the eldest daughter of a pawnbroker who lived by the inner gateway of the Zōjōji temple. Tomo had decided that the only arrangement likely to work would be with a tradesman's family more interested in property or social status than in personal character; for the first wife, too, she had chosen the daughter of a cloth merchant in Nihonbashi. Miya's family, who had already been told by the go-between about the Shirakawas' property and Yukitomo's career, only needed to hear that Takao would be brought up by his grandparents without troubling Miya in any way for both the mother and Miya's elder brother, now head of the family, to show immediate enthusiasm. For the moment the couple might have to live in rooms in the Shirakawas' house, but after Yukitomo's death the larger part of the income from a considerable number of buildings and estates within the city limits would fall to Michimasa, which was quite enough to make Miya's luxury-loving mother accept everything else—the previous wife, the stepchild, the fact that the bridegroom had no occupation. She was also much taken with the Shirakawas' suggestion that no trousseau would be necessary. For her bridal outfit, Miya was dressed in a red robe from the pawnshop, which was a good three or four inches shorter in the sleeve than the white silk under-kimono.

Since for her own daughter Etsuko's marriage Tomo had carefully chosen everything herself, from neckbands to the last undergarment, lest Etsuko's mother-in-law and relatives should see them and laugh at her when she went to live with them, she was shocked that a woman so smart in her personal appearance and so sophisticated in her speech as Miya's mother could show such casualness in providing for her child, and the reflection that it was precisely this outlook that had made it possible for the mother to give her yet unmarried daughter as second wife to a man like Michimasa reinforced the pity she felt for Miya.

"Ma'am . . ." said Suga after Miya had gone back to the main room where the wedding guests were waiting. She pointed to the white under-kimono that she had been folding after helping the bride change her costume in the rear room set apart for the purpose. Tomo frowned as she saw the light brown stain still visible on the garment, and said with quiet emphasis as she went out in Miya's wake:

"Don't tell the maids. You and Yumi fold them, please. It would be awful for Miya if she thought we'd noticed."

Meekly finishing her folding of the white robe, Suga was startled on glancing round to see Yumi, her hair done in a round bun, standing before the mirror with the red outer kimono discarded by Miya draped about her own shoulders.

"Yumi! Whatever are you up to!"

Tall, oval-faced, with heavy eyebrows like a youth, the Yumi in the mirror stared back and said:

"I suppose this is how I'd look if I was a bride. The effect's rather mannish, isn't it? I look as though I ought to be holding a halberd or something."

"Like Shizuka, the heroine in the Kabuki play," said Suga, taking up the joke with unusual alacrity. "But hurry up and take it off. If the mistress comes, you'll be in real trouble."

"Don't worry. The two geishas from Shimbashi have just started dancing the congratulatory dance, so they'll all be too busy watching. Here Suga—you try it on too. After all, it doesn't look as if we'll ever get any other chance to wear wedding clothes." As she spoke, she swiftly took off the long-sleeved outer garment and slipped it over Suga's shoulders. Trembling and fearful though she was, Suga did not remove it immediately but quietly got up and with a glance about her went and stood before the mirror as Yumi had done.

"It's so heavy! I don't have your look of breeding, so it doesn't suit me so well."

"Oh, but it does! You look pretty. It looks much better on you than it did just now on the young mistress."

"Really . . . ?" The tone was doubtful, but Suga did not seem displeased as she adjusted the neck of the garment and stared hard at her own face to which the crimson of the embroidered robe gave an added vividness. In both Suga and Yumi—the girl who had been bought for money and come as a concubine and the girl who had started as a maid and been elevated to concubinage

—there smouldered an unbearable envy of the showy trimmings of the wedding ceremony whereby a woman, amidst universal congratulation, became a lawful wife in the eyes of society; the envy was all the stronger in that they knew nothing of the world, having come as innocent girls, been initiated into womanhood by Shirakawa, and done their growing up all within the confines of this house.

"This kimono looks as though it came from the pawnshop. Look—the red silk inside the sleeve has faded," said Yumi, turning back Suga's long sleeve as she stood before her.

"It's been worn by somebody, hasn't it? I'm sure the bride who wore it before couldn't have been very happy, seeing that it got sent to the pawnshop."

"No more *this* bride," put in Suga, sighing as she slipped the heavy robe off her shoulders. She should not say such things on such an auspicious day, she felt, but a surge of resentment welled up in her against Michimasa and the contemptuous way he addressed her, as though she were some domestic animal.

"No indeed," took up Yumi promptly. "Marrying a man like him, and as his second wife too . . . Secondhand kimonos are the least you can expect. I'd refuse him if it were me! I wouldn't care how much money he had, or whether he was the only son or not— the very idea of marrying that half-witted misfit makes me shudder." She shook her body and grimaced as though she had found some unpleasant insect on her.

"I wonder why he was born that way, when the master and mistress are both brighter than average? The master once said it must be because he was born when the mistress was only fifteen, so he's not quite all there. He certainly couldn't be more different from the young lady he's marrying, could he?"

"Seki said the son's had to pay for all the women the father's deceived."

"Don't!"

Suga's thick eyebrows contracted and her face darkened. For Yumi, the words passed her lips lightly without further thought, but for Suga they were less easily forgotten, persisting like evil spirits, with overtones of curses and unforgotten grudges. To hear Yumi talking of such portentous matters in such an utterly care-free manner made Suga feel a kind of self-disgust: she reminded herself of a ditch that would not allow things to flow through smoothly but became clogged with filth.

For a few days following the wedding ceremony Tomo watched in distress as Miya went about silent and uncommunicative, with the pale, withered look of a flower touched by the wind. Even Yukitomo, knowing women as he did, seemed to be disturbed at the idea of the harm both spiritual and physical that Michimasa's unbridled speech and action might be inflicting on Miya in the privacy of the marriage chamber, and instead of turning aside with an open look of displeasure as he normally did when he saw his son he took pains to placate him by giving him the Swiss-style gold watch with a platinum chain that he had long coveted and by ordering Western-style food from distant restaurants in order to gratify Michimasa's taste for the unusual. He knew well that with Michimasa it would be less effective to lecture him on how to cherish his new wife than to please him with food or gifts, which always improved his temper visibly and, if hardly making him delightful company, at least stopped him from distressing his wife with nonsensical remarks.

As expected, Michimasa cheered up in his own vacant way, and as he did so Miya began once more to laugh out loud, narrowing her eyes in mirth till they threatened to disappear completely in her soft cheeks.

Although in photographs Miya did not have the well-defined

91

outlines that would have made her a beauty of Suga's or Yumi's type, the soft flesh was delicately molded on the slender frame, and the skin on her face, arms, and legs had an even blush of pale pink like cherry blossom. When a smile appeared in her narrow eyes and at the corners of her slightly loose, passive mouth she acquired an indescribable charm and even an equivocal, perishable type of beauty. Perhaps because of her slender build her movements were light and graceful, and her lilting speech with its slight plebeian twang brought a rare touch of gaiety to the bureaucratic solemnity of the Shirakawa residence.

It was Tomo who first fell in love with Miya's ingratiating femininity. The familiar way in which, as they were setting off home after the meeting arranged by the go-between, Miya had said, "Mother, your jacket—" and gone round to turn down her collar for her had had a warmth that inspired Tomo with the hope that such a daughter-in-law might help lower the barrier of stiffness with which she was always obliged to surround herself so carefully at home. The sense of magical promise was almost like the first moments of love between man and woman, and Tomo had prayed eagerly that the match might be realized. Her daughter Etsuko, who had married last year, had been reared as a jewel without a flaw, yet Tomo sensed in her something of the cold, hard quality of crystal; and Suga's gloomily reticent expression, the eyes that were forever sullen and suspicious like a beautiful cat's, grew more disturbing as she got older. Yumi, the most outgoing of them all, was merely free from reserve, as clearcut and superficially gay as the branches and blossom of the peach tree, and was quite remote from that romantic, sensuous mood for which Tomo longed. As the two concubines formed an increasingly impenetrable barrier between herself and Yukitomo, physical relations between them had ceased altogether, and though the faith in the saving powers of Amida that her mother back home in the country had sought to bequeath to her was, little by little, beginning to put forth buds in her daily life, she was only just forty and healthy still in mind and body, so that fight it though she might the desire for the warm contact of a human body welled up in her irresistibly.

Since her code of morals would have considered it a sin to take a lover so long as she had a husband in Yukitomo, her sexual desire may unconsciously have been deflected to the same sex, so that she looked at Miya not with a woman's eyes but with the eyes of a desiring man, seeking all unawares the enveloping softness, free of all sharp angles, that only a woman could offer. Miya had happened to fit in with the image of a feminine woman that Tomo was seeking.

One further reason why Tomo had hoped to get Miya as a second wife for Michimasa was her concern for her grandchild Takao. Takao had lost his mother shortly after birth; Tomo had been obliged to rear him herself, and her search for some object to love had been concentrated on the child. His innocent baby face, smiling despite its ignorance of a mother, had inspired her with a boundless compassion and a sense of life endlessly renewed.

Tomo, burdened with a constant sense of guilt at her inability to love her own son Michimasa, would sometimes gaze at her grandchild's limbs as he romped about so full of life and marvel that she could feel so much affection for Michimasa's child. In Yukitomo's eyes, too, Takao could do no wrong, though when Michimasa and Etsuko were in their infancy Yukitomo had been disturbed by the children and had often sent them with his wife to some distant part of the house so that he would not be irritated by the sound of their crying. Yukitomo would take him from Maki and holding him in with both hands lift him up high in the air. "Fly, Takao, fly, high up in the sky!" he would chant, and roar with laughter. Since Yukitomo showed such affection for him, both Suga and Yumi also made much of the "little master," and Takao was passed from the arms of one member of the household to another, a constant focus of attention. So long as Takao was with them, Yukitomo would speak to Tomo with his old lack of reserve and even Tomo could talk without any sense of barrier. This child, offspring of their own unworthy son Michimasa, was a silent witness to the blood ties that existed between the two of them, now husband and wife in name alone. This idea too had been instilled in Tomo's lonely soul by her own mother who had died in Kumamoto the previous year, shortly before Takao's birth, and Tomo cherished it accordingly. So fond of Takao was Yukitomo that it was already decided that whatever other children Michimasa might have Takao would remain legitimate heir to the Shirakawa estate, one part of which had already been made over into his name. Thus Takao's position in the family was in no danger so long as his grandparents were alive; but they might die unexpectedly, and Tomo instinctively feared for Takao's sake to introduce a woman of strong character as Michimasa's second wife. On this score, too, Miya passed the test.

Before a month had passed Miya was on cheerful, friendly terms with everybody in the house. She made no conscious effort, yet seemed to distil so sweet, so flowerlike a fragrance that not only Yukitomo and Tomo but even Suga and Yumi, who might have been expected to feel jealousy towards another young woman, would watch her with frank, unguarded smiles. She would peer into Takao's face as he lay in Maki's arms and exclaim, "How sweet! Let me hold him for a while!" and taking him in her slender arms kiss him unaffectedly on the cheek, laughing till her eyes became the merest creases in her face. Yukitomo and Tomo were delighted by her apparent complete unawareness of the predecessor who had borne Takao.

On fine days Miya would gaze out from the second floor over the sea off Shinagawa and rejoice like a child: it was so cheerful here in this house on the hill, she said, after her own home which was shut in on every side by other dwellings.

Miya was reputed to be good at singing ballads in the *tokiwazu* style, so one evening they had her sing the ballad of the unhappy lovers Osono and Rokusa on their way to die together. Yumi, who was trained in the same *tokiwazu* style, accompanied her on the samisen. Gradually, as she gently related the dialogue of the doomed couple in a voice that was strong and steady yet full of feminine charm, her eyebrows began to contract and her white throat to strain in strangled sobs, till despite themselves the listeners were half persuaded that Miya herself had become Osono, and were overcome by a kind of sensuous sorrow. Coming to the end of the scene, Miya was combing back the loose strands of hair and wiping her damp forehead with a handkerchief when Michimasa, who had drunk too much saké, vomited copiously on the *tatami* and was carried out into the anteroom.

Frowning, Miya made reluctantly to get up, but when Yukitomo told her to leave it to the maids she looked pleased and came happily to sit by her father-in-law's side.

"Let me help you to some saké. My awful singing has made the young master sick," she said, holding the china bottle poised on her upturned palm in a seductive manner that came as a vague shock to Tomo sitting next to her, so much did it remind her of a young and newly qualified geisha.

"Nonsense," he said. "Your singing almost made me feel like the hero of a love suicide myself. Everybody's sitting very quiet, aren't they? Here, now, have a drink. Somehow I think you're a good drinker."

He gave her his own saké cup and filled it to the brim for her. Ever since she came as a bride she had refrained from indulging her taste for saké, but now at Yukitomo's instigation she drank several cupfuls in succession, so that her eyes grew faintly pink at the corners and her face acquired so much the air of a full-blown flower that Suga could not help drawing Yumi's attention to it with a meaningful glance.

Observing Miya without appearing to do so, Yukitomo gradually realized that whether she was at home or out it was the times when Michimasa was not there that showed her cheerful youthfulness at its most radiant and allowed her to be herself, as gay and carefree as a butterfly. When her husband Michimasa was with her, and Tomo and the others thoughtfully went away in order to leave the young couple to themselves, she would look disconsolate and, finding some excuse to leave him before long, would go and join Suga and the others in attendance upon Yukitomo.

On one occasion Yukitomo deliberately sent Michimasa to replace him at a garden party given by a cement firm, and in his absence took Suga and Yumi, and Miya with them, to see the irises in the famous garden at Horikiri, leaving Tomo to take care of the house.

The spacious lake of the iris garden was crossed by numerous bridges of narrow planks arranged to form zigzags across the water, and the entire surface was covered with the dark green leaves of the irises whose gay purple, white, and dappled blooms swayed in the breezes of early summer. Swallows skimmed the surface of the water with flashes of their white underbellies. The beauty of the three young women, in their varying hairstyles and with their kimonos of many cloths and colors, was so startling that it drew glances from the other visitors they passed on their way.

"It's like looking at an old color print," said one old woman gazing at them enthralled, "to see three such fine women standing together among the irises."

Of the three it was Miya who frolicked most gaily of all; when the planks of the bridge creaked beneath her clogs it was she who cried "Oh! It's going to break!" in exaggerated alarm and clung fearfully to Suga and Yumi. When they went up the bank again, Yukitomo helped Miya up, almost lifting her light body in his arms and recalling as he did so how once among the apprentice geishas of Shimbashi there had been a girl with just such a lithe body as this.

"The young mistress doesn't seem a bit lonely even when she's away from the young master, does she?" said Suga casually that evening in Yukitomo's bedroom. "She looks younger, in fact— almost like a young girl."

In the ten years that she had served him as mistress Suga had learned the art of probing in the most innocent way possible into the secret recesses of Yukitomo's mind. Perhaps he did not sense the subtle inquiry concealed in Suga's words, for he made no reply but sat with an ambiguous smile playing about the corners of his mouth.

"What are you smiling at? Stop it!"

"It's all right—it's not you, it's Miya."

"The young mistress? What about her?"

"Doesn't her face when she laughs remind you of something?"

"Not that I've noticed."

"The women in those erotic prints. Remember? I showed them to you once, didn't I?"

"Well! Of all the—" Suga reddened.

"That kind of woman may be all right as a wife for a semiidiot like Michimasa, but . . ." He left the rest to her imagination and putting an arm around the shoulders that were cool and white as newly fallen snow drew her to him. She snuggled up to him

97

docilely, convinced by his unspoken comment, it seemed, of the scorn in which he held Miya.

Tomo's fears had not after all been unfounded.

Perhaps because of the unusual fierceness of the summer, Miya, who had been troubled with pleurisy as a girl and was excessively susceptible to the heat, became a semiinvalid, losing weight visibly and spending half the time in bed upstairs. Then, one morning around the time when the first cool breezes were beginning to blow, an alarming noise came from upstairs where the young couple lived. Miya came rushing down the stairs, almost falling over herself in her haste, and nearly collided with Tomo in the corridor.

"Mother . . ." she gasped, and suddenly burst out weeping in a loud voice. Upstairs, Michimasa could be heard stamping on the floor and yelling imprecations, but no one made to go up to him. Startled though she was, Tomo had been expecting that this day would come sooner or later. Putting her arms about the shivering, uncontrollably sobbing Miya she led her into a room at the back of the house and tried, almost apologetically, to calm her down while seeking to elicit the details of her quarrel with Michimasa.

At first Miya could get out nothing between her sobs but "Oh what a fool I was . . . I can't stand it . . . I can't stay with him any longer," but as the storm of emotion passed she began, albeit incoherently, to complain of Michimasa's heartless behavior. As Tomo had suspected, she had found him somehow unsympathetic from the start, but her illness this summer had shown her still more clearly the callousness of his nature. Far from worrying himself over her physical debility he sought to have physical relations with her almost every night. She had given in, since to object only made him more insistent, but in the last few days she had been menstruating. At such times she normally refused him, but this time nothing would make him take no for an answer. The previous night she had finally refused him absolutely, but in the morning he had been terrifyingly out of temper, had told her among other things that a wife who disobeyed her husband's commands was punishable by law, and had thrown at her everything he could lay his hands on. If she stayed married to such a man, she would surely end up by getting killed, she said, so she was going back to her parents' home that very day. Even allowing for a certain hysterical exaggeration, a man like Michimasa was quite capable of the things she described, and Tomo listened with complete sympathy; yet even so she did her utmost to persuade Miya not to leave the house into which she had married, insisting that they would speak to Michimasa and see that he never committed such outrages again.

The Miya that Tomo had pictured to herself was a gentle woman ruled by her affections, but today she was a different person altogether. Her face was blank, hard, and drained of all color, and the almond eyes that normally smiled so tenderly were narrowed at the outer corners and expressionless. Tomo tried to arouse in her a kind of fellow-feeling by talking of her own feelings as a woman in the face of the indignities she must constantly suffer from Yukitomo, but Miya seemed deaf and indifferent to such difficult, depressing talk and only dwelt more and more insistently on her own unhappy married life, as though it were all Tomo's own responsibility. Sensing that the more she talked the more Miya saw her as a country woman wrapped up in the past, Tomo was overcome by a profound disappointment. As it was gradually borne in on her that despite appearances Miya was not the essentially warm-hearted woman who brought a little grace to other people's lives that she had imagined, she felt an increasing irritation at her own lack of insight.

Leaving the room after urging Miya once more to give the

matter further thought, Tomo had an uneasy foreboding that the affair would make Yukitomo angry with Michimasa and Miya, so that once again he would vent his spleen on herself. It was Yukitomo's habit whenever Michimasa created some unpleasantness to attack Tomo as though Michimasa were her child and not his own as well.

But Yukitomo, who in one of his good moods had taken Maki out into the garden to show Takao the red dragonflies dancing about the new heads of pampas grass, handed the child back to Maki when he saw Tomo's face and came back to the veranda.

"So Michimasa's done it again, eh?" he said with a wry smile before Tomo could say anything. "It seems Miya's threatening to go back to her parents . . ." Either Suga or Yumi had apparently already reported the outlines of the affair, but Tomo nevertheless gave him an account in meticulous detail.

Yukitomo nodded as he listened, then when Tomo had finished suggested in a mild tone that rather than complain to Michimasa it would be better to send him to Echigo for a month or so to see the oilfield there, in order to give the domestic quarrel time to blow over. A relative of theirs who worked for the company was leaving for Kashiwazaki the next day, so he could be asked to take along Michimasa, who could do the sights of Niigata and perhaps Sado Island, and at the same time be gently initiated by the relative, who was a man of the world, into the art of handling a wife. Michimasa himself might possibly benefit a little thereby and it would also give Miya a chance to have second thoughts. Michimasa, who was fond of seeing unfamiliar places, was certain to be delighted. Tomo was impressed by the good sense of her husband's plan. She looked at him with new hope: now that they had found a wife for Michimasa, perhaps even Yukitomo, who normally regarded his son as the bane of his existence, would feel a more natural affection for him.

For two or three days after Michimasa had left on his journey, Miya kept to her room complaining that she felt unwell, but the absence of the other party to the quarrel must have taken the fight out of her for she said nothing more about returning to her parents' home.

"Here, Miya," said Yukitomo in a hearty voice as he flung open the sliding doors and came in to sit by the bed where Miya's small face, innocent of all cosmetics, rested against the pillow. "I'm thinking of taking Maki and Takao to Enoshima and staying the night. Why don't you come with us?"

Miya sat up as though cheered by the youthfulness of his voice.

"Enoshima . . . how lovely!" she said, already tying the girdle around her narrow, girlish waist. "I love all those souvenir shops selling shell-work!"

By the time they arrived home from Enoshima, Miya had completely recovered her spirits. Her face beamed with its accustomed charm and she was at her most amusing as she told them how skillfully a fisherman at Chigo-ga-fuchi had dived into the sea to bring up abalones and turbos for them, or how at a souvenir shop Takao had coveted the biggest conch shell of all and had had it put to his tiny mouth to blow.

She even came to Tomo's room and bowed meekly to the floor.

"I'm sorry I lost my temper the other day," she said. "But I shan't be causing you any more worry from now on . . ."

Yukitomo came as Tomo was bouncing Takao on her knee and himself broached the subject:

"It seems Miya's going to stay put. And I told her that we'd keep a firm hand on Michimasa for her."

When Michimasa himself came home about ten days later, even he seemed to treat Miya with more amiability than before, and many times laughter was to be heard from their room when they were alone together. Yukitomo seemed to be pleased that the young couple were on such good terms.

Yet although the storm seemed more or less to have subsided, in Tomo's mind there always remained, silly and ugly, a picture of Miya's agitated face with its narrowed eyes as she had attacked her that day, a picture all the more vivid for the image of the charming, seemingly warmhearted girl that she had cherished until then.

On the night of the twenty-sixth day of the seventh month, according to an old tradition, good fortune would favor the first person to catch sight of the slender first-quarter moon rising in the late-night eastern sky, and it was the custom for large numbers of people to gather to await the moon on high places whence its rising was visible. As it rose, it was believed, three Buddhist deities—Amida, with his attendants Kannon and Seishi—were to be seen riding in its boat-shaped, luminous crescent.

The Shirakawas' house looking out eastward over the sea was an ideal spot for awaiting the moon, and Yukitomo, with his love of gaiety and his fondness for using such occasions to hold lively drinking parties for relatives and friends or to organize games of chance for their amusement, had invited a dozen or more men and women to join him that night in two second-floor rooms thrown open for the purpose at the front of the house. Some were playing "flower cards," some played *go*, some as they gossiped were helping themselves liberally to the snacks provided with the saké; all of them were pleasurably excited at being able to participate without the slightest sense of guilt, on the pretext of awaiting the moonrise, in this kind of late-night frivolity.

Occasionally a guest would peer out at the dark sky as though suddenly remembering their ostensible aim, only to turn again to where the cards were being slapped in rapid succession on the *tatami*.

102

"I wonder if it isn't time for the moon to rise? It must be after one."

"Not for a long while yet. The papers said the moon would rise at one thirty-five."

"I only hope it doesn't cloud over just then . . ."

Tomo went downstairs to tell the servants to bring fresh supplies of food. On her way to the kitchen she glanced into the room where Takao was supposed to be sleeping and saw Maki bent forward beside the quilts where Takao lay in bed, talking intently in a low voice to Suga and Yumi.

They broke off abruptly at the sight of Tomo, the expression on the faces of all three so comically confused that Tomo had an immediate intuition, like an electric shock, of what was wrong.

On her way back from the kitchen she found Suga lurking like a shadow at the foot of the stairs.

"Ma'am . . ." she said in voice of suppressed pain.

"What's the matter, Suga? What were you talking about with Maki?" Even as she spoke, by a kind of tacit agreement, they took themselves out onto the deserted veranda.

The light from the unshuttered rooms on the second floor upstairs threw the garden shrubs into dim green relief and the loud voices and laughter reached them with startling immediacy. The late-night autumn air struck the skin like a cold spray of water.

"Ma'am, I was really shocked . . . that the young mistress . . ."

Suga got so far, then her voice expired in a kind of wheeze. Fighting against the darkness that threatened to steal over her vision, Tomo put both arms around Suga's trembling shoulders.

"I know . . . You mean, something happened that time at Enoshima . . ."

"Yes, Maki . . . Maki saw with her own eyes . . ."

Her teeth chattering all the while, Suga repeated what she had heard from Maki that evening. Miya had kept Yukitomo company over his saké and had herself drunk her fill, then, complaining that the noise of the waves scared her, she had had her bed laid out in the same room as Maki and Takao and, too far gone even to be got out of her kimono and into her nightwear, had finally been put to bed by Maki and a maid so that they could clear the things away in the main room.

Yukitomo went to bed in the back room, separated from the others only by a pair of sliding doors. Tired from the day's exertions Maki had slept soundly, but awoke with a start to find the night still dark and the waves beating on the rocks below, roaring with the ferocity of a storm. Peering at the next bed by the faint light of the bedside lamp, she found the quilts in which Miya supposedly lay in a drunken stupor quite empty, while from the room at the rear, fitfully between the roar of the waves as they advanced and retreated, she could hear Miya's voice strangely seductive and nasal, whether crying or laughing she could not tell . . . Several times Maki had doubted her own ears and told herself it was all a dream, but the intimate sounds from the rear room had continued, murmuring on and on till close to daybreak.

"Tonight, too . . . the young mistress said she had a cold and went to the separate wing alone . . ."

Again Suga broke off. Yukitomo had excused himself a while ago; he had doubtless gone surreptitiously to join her there.

Tomo had a mental image of Michimasa's eyes staring vacant and motionless from his smooth, pallid face as he played *go* upstairs with one of the guests, and a shudder raised goose pimples on her skin. Who could tell what dreadful things might occur should Michimasa get wind of what was happening? She was appalled at her own näiveté in assuming, despite her countless bitter experiences on account of Yukitomo's lechery, that within himself he still maintained the same moral code as herself. Without so much as a second thought he had trampled into the forbidden territory of his own son's marriage. For Yukitomo, no woman was anything more than a female of the species; and in that sense, of course, Miya must be a far more attractive female than either Suga or even Yumi . . . Nonetheless it was with a seething indignation quite different from the jealousy she had experienced when Yukitomo had first turned his affections to Suga and Yumi that Tomo now listened to Suga's complaint. The feeling was equally remote from both marital love and marital hatred, a fierce wrath that stood up to Yukitomo, the ungovernable male, and took beneath its protective wing Suga, Yumi, and even the offending Miya herself.

"Here it comes, here it comes . . . !"

"There it is—look, the moon of the twenty-sixth night!"

A confused clamor of voices, a trampling of feet on the veranda upstairs. Tomo too looked out over the sea, where even from this downstairs room the slender crescent of the moon was visible like an upturned eyebrow emerging in a faint glow from the surface of the water. With a sense of wonder, Tomo recalled how she had been told as a child that the forms of Amida and his two divine attendants were visible to the faithful, borne upon that thin golden semicircle. Was it really nonsense, that the shining forms of the Trinity, riding on the rays of moonlight, should manifest themselves to men's eyes? No—just occasionally, Tomo felt, it must be true, for the present world was too ugly, too full of sorrow. Yet as she gazed at the moon it was no Buddha-figure that emerged from its light, but two white butterflies fluttering close about each other in the pale-shining haze.

Purple Ribbon

The tradesmen and others who came to the house all said that the family Buddhist shrine was pitifully small for such a large establishment.

It may have been a relic from the unsettled days of their younger years, when Shirakawa was a government official obliged to move about the provinces from assignment to assignment and they had had to carry about with them the urn containing the ashes of his mother, who had died in the snow country where he was working at the time. Whatever the case, the sliding doors next to the cupboard containing the small shrine concealed a black lacquer safe emblazoned with the family crest in gold, and it was Tomo's custom to carry out all business and calculations relating to rents on houses and land in this Buddhist retreat tucked away at the back of the house. They had an acre or so each of land in Shiba, Nihonbashi, and Shitaya, of which some seventy percent was built on. The land rents and other dues came to quite a large figure, but defaulters were correspondingly common, and sometimes it was necessary to have recourse to the courts in order to reach a settlement. Supervision was no easy task. Each estate had its agent, but to leave everything to them invariably meant oversights, so once a month without fail Tomo would herself go to hear from the agents a detailed account of the state of the leased land and houses.

The man who now sat facing Tomo across the writing table in front of the safe was not an agent but Tomeji Iwamoto, who functioned as a kind of secretary for her. The son of Tomo's elder sister by a different mother, he had come to Tokyo from Kumamoto a few years earlier, counting on Shirakawa to find him a job.

He could handle correspondence and calculations, and his earnest, unassuming character had earned him the confidence of both Shirakawa and Tomo, who as the necessity arose would ask Iwamoto to undertake troublesome negotiations and legal business that could not be left to the agents.

Finishing a letter to a tenant who had left his rent unpaid for more than a year and in addition was demanding compensation for removal, Iwamoto handed a copy to Tomo. Carefully she read through the letter in the fine, well-written characters that contrasted so oddly with his short, thickset appearance, then said:

"Thank you. Things are much easier for me nowadays, now that I have you to write these for me. This kind of letter is too much for a woman, and your uncle can't be bothered with such matters."

One side of her mouth lifted in a smile, and she took up her pipe for the first time since the interview had started.

"How is your business? Does it look as though you'll get more customers?"

"Yes—one mustn't complain, I suppose. Only the other day we had an order from the supplies office of the Finance Ministry for quite a large number of wicker baskets for keeping papers in; two of the lads and myself went at it frantically and just managed to get them done in time."

All the while Iwamoto spoke, in his slow halting way with the provincial accent that had never left him, the good-natured smile never once deserted his face. Last year, again with the Shirakawas' help, he had started a small business selling boxes and hampers in the Tamuracho district of Shiba. He was unusually skillful with his hands and back home in the country was said to have woven the hampers to hold the trousseaus of all the brides in the neighborhood, so the Shirakawas had provided capital for the business in the expectation that it would not do too badly in a field where there was little competition.

"Really? Well, that's very good. It seems it takes a few years for a business to build up a clientele, so keep hard at it, won't you."

"I will. Why, it's you I have to thank for everything, so the least I can do is to work hard to repay your kindness."

Tomo, the short pipe between her teeth, had been steadily surveying Iwamoto as he sat with his hands on his knees, bobbing his head up and down like a bear.

"It's about time you got married and settled down, isn't it?" she said suddenly as though half to herself.

"There's nobody would have a man like me."

He smiled and wriggled uncomfortably, but his dark-skinned features flushed in a clumsy betrayal of feeling.

"Of course they will. Any number of them, if only you look properly . . ." She broke off, her face thoughtful. For a while she was silent, smoking her pipe as though in two minds about something, till finally Iwamoto seemed to feel uncomfortable and tidying up the papers on the table said stiffly, squaring his elbows and bowing his head:

"Well, then, I'll be off. Please send for me if you want anything done."

"Why—do you have to go? Have you got a lot to do today?"

"No . . . the shop's not—"

"Then sit down, please. You see, on this question of your marriage there's something I wanted to ask you about."

Tomo pushed the table to one side and moved the brazier beside her slightly closer to Iwamoto.

"Here, warm yourself up."

"Thank you."

"The thing is, you see . . . Now, this is just between ourselves, but does the girl you marry have to be untouched?"

"Eh?" Iwamoto blinked his large eyes dubiously and stared into Tomo's face.

"I mean, would you object to a woman who came second-hand?"

"Secondhand? You mean . . . someone who'd been married already?"

"Yes . . . well, not exactly *married*, but . . ."

She broke off and spent a while poking at the charcoal in the brazier with a brass poker. Eventually she looked up again and said:

"Actually, I'm thinking of Yumi . . ."

"Yumi . . . ?" echoed Iwamoto, then sat staring vacantly at some point in the distance.

A while earlier, as he had come in through the side entrance and walked along the corridor that skirted the front rooms, he had seen Yumi and Suga sitting facing each other, arranging aspidistras in a bronze vase.

"Is the master out?" he had asked.

"He's gone over to the new house at Tsunamachi," replied Yumi in a clear voice, snapping away busily with her scissors. "With Master Takao and his nurse . . . Yes, I expect he'll stay there tonight."

The house at Tsunamachi was the house where Michimasa had gone to live the previous year. Suga merely bowed and murmured something inaudible without looking up from the dark green leaves of the aspidistras. Yumi might lack conscious charm, he had thought, but she was more lively and straightforward than Suga, who always seemed somehow heavy and remote. His head in a whirl at Tomo's unexpected proposal, he found himself

109

recalling the impression and somehow began to feel nervous.

Iwamoto was still looking startled as Tomo began to explain from the beginning about Yumi's background and the circumstances that had made her available for marriage.

For generations, Yumi's family had served as chief retainers to a petty feudal lord known as Toda, but ever since the Meiji Restoration they had lived a life of poverty. Yumi had come to the Shirakawa home as a maid at the age of sixteen but had eventually become Shirakawa's concubine in the same way as Suga before her, whereupon a considerable sum of money had almost certainly been handed over to her parents. In exchange, Yukitomo had had her name transferred to the Shirakawa family register as their adopted daughter, just as he had done with Suga. Yukitomo might well have intended this as a kind of pledge that he was not going to amuse himself with a respectable girl then abandon her after a short while, but it was a blot on the family register that a woman marked down as an adopted daughter should in fact be a concubine, and Tomo, moreover, disliked the suggestion of a cruel design to impose restraints in advance on Suga and Yumi in case they should ever be attracted to men other than Yukitomo himself.

Yumi's elder sister Shin, whose husband had been adopted into their family but had since left her a widow, had come to call on them at the New Year and had suggested that Yumi should be released, asking Tomo in strict confidence to exert her influence. Since Shin had no children, the family line would die out unless something was done soon, she said. Yumi had been in service for nearly ten years by now, so she would like, provided the master agreed, to take her away, find her a husband, and raise one of the offspring as her own.

"I ought to adopt a child, of course," she added, "but our

family is in no position to do that, so I decided in the end it would be better to get her married."

"Does Yumi herself agree to this?" Tomo had asked.

"Well yes . . ." The reply was vague, but Tomo could imagine more or less the kind of thing that Yumi had said to her sister.

The following afternoon, Tomo had asked Suga to help her get some furniture out of the storehouse. Yumi was preparing some Chinese ink in the living room for Yukitomo, who had writing to do, so it had been quite natural for Suga to answer the summons.

When Suga, at her directions, had finished getting the boxes containing small tables and soup bowls down from their shelves, Tomo asked her about Yumi. Although jealousy might have been expected between concubines of the same man, they had never shown any sign of rivalry for his affections. Perhaps it was because they were both young enough to be his children. Yet grateful though she was for the sisterliness that kept the household free of strife, there were times when Tomo could not help wondering at the meekness with which the two young women accepted their lot. For that same reason, though, she felt it wiser in a case like the present one to use Suga as an intermediary in ascertaining Yukitomo's and Yumi's true feelings.

Kneeling on the matting with a box containing a small lacquered table still in front of her, Suga lowered her thick eyelashes as she listened to Tomo, then said in a dismal voice:

"The master would agree. I believe he was the one who first suggested that Yumi should leave and settle down in her own home."

Her face as she sat with the sunlight falling on her back was in shadow, the large eyes alone gleaming with a mournful light. Tomo had the illusion that Suga was blaming her for something.

"From the very beginning I don't think the master was as fond of Yumi as he was of you . . . I don't suppose that's changed lately has it?"

"Me . . .?" Suga stirred lethargically and rubbed her hands on her knees as she spoke. "It doesn't matter about me. But Yumi's such a lively girl. I expect she's got tired of always being a 'second woman.' "

Suga's low tones as she uttered the words "second woman" had a leaden quality that struck home forcefully to Tomo's heart. Whenever she heard the phrase, Tomo was reminded vividly of the time when at Yukitomo's command she had gone to Tokyo, found the young Suga, and brought her back to Fukushima where her husband worked. For the change from the charming young victim to the apathetic Suga of today, dull as a silkworm's cocoon, there lay a responsibility that could not, Tomo felt, be attributed to her husband alone.

"*We* are resigned to being 'second women,' but when people who aren't supposed to be like us start behaving in the same way, I think it's terrible."

A great tear splashed down from Suga's heavy-lidded eyes and fell on her knee. Looking down, she covered it with her finger and remained with head bowed.

"I know—you mean Tsunamachi, don't you? You don't know how much that's worried me too. I thought perhaps you'd understand at least a little."

Tomo sighed, her gaze resting on Suga's finger as though she resented the tear.

Suga was referring to Yukitomo's infatuation with his daughter-in-law Miya. Miya had stayed with them in the big house until she had safely borne her first child, a period of several years during which Tomo had suffered agonies at the thought of the trouble that would occur should Michimasa ever realize the relationship between his father and his wife. Since she was too far

112

estranged from Yukitomo herself to do anything, she had said any number of times to Suga:

"I'd like you to keep an eye on them. Miya is one case where nothing can be done openly about the relationship, so I look to you and Yumi to see he doesn't get too fond of her."

Each time, Suga had shaken her head fiercely.

"What can *I* do about it?" she demanded balefully. "The young mistress is the type that was born to be a geisha or a courtesan. She knows exactly how to make the master fond of her, and how to play up to him. Yumi and I are no match for her."

Like most men of an amorous nature Yukitomo seemed in fact to find a particular stimulus in an illicit affair, and was showing for Miya a passion no less intense than he had shown for Suga in those early days after he first made her his own. Miya too seemed far happier to be loved by her father-in-law, with his skill in dealing with women, than by her ineffectual and degenerate husband, and whenever Yukitomo had Suga or Yumi by him and was distant in his manner she would become noticeably bad-tempered and vent her feelings on Tomo and Suga.

Things had eventually become too much, apparently, even for Yukitomo, who on Tomo's indirectly given advice had last year moved the young married couple to Tsunamachi in the Mita district, where he could go to visit them from time to time. When he went he always took with him Takao and Takao's nurse. At such times Michimasa would receive a generous allowance of pocket money from his father and would go off happily to the theater or on an overnight trip. The nurse and the maids too would go off elsewhere to amuse themselves, bearing the baby with them. That left Yukitomo and Miya alone together. The women might realize what was afoot, but the unexpectedly generous tips made them if anything look forward to the visits of the master from the big house, while Michimasa, provided he

113

was doing something he liked, was like a small child with not the slightest suspicion concerning the relationship between his father and his wife.

Much of this had reached the ears of Suga and Yumi via Takao's nurse and Maki, and thanks largely to Suga were conveyed in turn to Tomo.

At first Tomo had echoed sympathetically Suga's indirect complaints, but realizing that at such times Suga later confided Tomo's half of the conversation to Yukitomo, whose bad temper was thereupon vented upon her own unsuspecting self, she had taken of late to brushing aside any tales that Suga came bearing.

Now that he was within sight of sixty the presence of Yumi, for whom he had never cared as he had for Suga, was undoubtedly more of a burden than otherwise for Yukitomo. Without seeming to do so, he was hinting that Yumi should leave and become a respectable married woman, and Yumi herself was of like mind: so much at least Tomo gathered from Suga's ponderous speech that always sounded as though she had something lodged in her back teeth.

If Yukitomo and Yumi felt that way, no one could complain if Yumi took herself off the Shirakawa register and returned to her own family. Provided they added a sum of money corresponding to the clothes and personal effects that had been made for her during the past everybody should be satisfied. And yet ... At this point, a new thought struck the wary Tomo.

Supposing Yumi went back to her parents and got married, would she refrain from talking to her husband of the illicit liaison between Miya and Yukitomo? It would not matter so much if she were an ordinary servant, but for such a story to be told by a woman who had been in their household for so long, supposedly as an adopted daughter, could do the Shirakawa name nothing but harm.

If she was to be married off anyway, would it not be possible to find somewhere where she would be inseparably associated with the family? Considering every possibility in turn, Tomo suddenly remembered someone unexpectedly close at hand—her nephew Iwamoto. Of course Iwamoto, now, would probably agree to any suggestion she made.

Precisely because he was perfectly aware that Yumi was Yukitomo's concubine, he would also know that the concubines in the Shirakawa household were by way of being housekeepers who could sew and cook, and he should be well acquainted with Yumi's easy-going, almost masculine nature. Above all, he was familiar with her attractive, refined oval face and the ample clothes and domestic articles that were unquestionably too good for a man of his present standing. Tomo broached the subject with Iwamoto with a ninety-percent confidence that he would agree. If Yumi objected, of course, that would be the end of it, but Tomo knew from long years of observation in the same household that Yumi was not by nature choosy.

As expected, Iwamoto fell in happily with Tomo's skillfully phrased effort at matchmaking. Born in Kumamoto into the family of a samurai with a small stipend, and accustomed from childhood to hearing tales of attendants receiving as wives serving-women whom the lord had already deflowered, or of chief retainers' concubines being married off to lower-ranking samurai, Iwamoto had no sense of either insult or disgust at the idea of taking in marriage a woman who had been mistress of a man to whom he was obliged both as uncle and as benefactor.

Yumi's own family too were delighted that the Shirakawas should show so much concern over what happened to their daughter, since a marriage to Iwamoto, who was Mrs. Shirakawa's nephew, would mean a new and close tie with the family. Yumi was young enough to be Shirakawa's daughter, and in addition to the wife there was another concubine called Suga who had preceded her, so her position in the household had from the outset been more like that of a chambermaid. In appearance, though, she had a refinement that fitted her better than Suga to be mistress of a household and, together with the absence of the pettiness and suspicion so often found in women, saved her from any trace of the shadow that usually hung over a concubine.

In the same way Yumi herself agreed without fuss to the match with Iwamoto. Since she had often talked and laughed about Iwamoto's clumsy Kyushu speech and his prim, methodical movements, Suga found it strange that these should bother her so little now that she was going to marry him, and said to Yukitomo:

"I wonder whether Yumi will make a go of it with Mr. Iwamoto?"

"Don't worry," said Yukitomo, carelessly, a smile obviously free of all ill-feeling creasing his cheeks, on which faint liver spots were visible. "Yumi could settle down with anybody."

"Nothing seems to bother you, does it?" said Suga in a disgruntled tone, fixing Yukitomo with a gloomy stare.

"Do *you* want to get married too? I expect you get tired of tending to the needs of an old man like me, don't you?"

"I don't have the initiative for anything else anyway . . ."

Her tone was casual but she itched with frustration at not being able to give voice to the angry thoughts that came thrusting up within her: "I can't expect to do like the young mistress, anyway"; "After all, you never taught me how to deceive men like she can"; "I don't have *that* kind of skill, which is why I have to go on getting older, without a home of my own, under the thumb of a straitlaced woman like the mistress." Although she seemed to have her own way with him, Yukitomo was in a sense both father and master for her, too important a being in her life for her not to fear using sharp words that might strike home where it hurt.

When she called to mind Miya's lighthearted manner, how she quite shamelessly made up to Yukitomo with her gay, cheerful expressions, her innocent fits of helpless laughter and the gentle, slightly nasal tone in which she called him "Papa," Suga was not free from jealousy of a kind, yet it did not seem like the jealousy of a woman whose lover had been lured into bed by another.

On the night before Yumi was to go back to her parents' home the two of them with Yukitomo's permission set out their quilts side by side in the same room.

As they talked they gazed nostalgically at each other's faces looming pale in the dim light of the bedside lamps, their necks supported on wooden pillows to protect their elaborate hairstyles.

March was near its close. Outside, a drizzling rain fell silently and the night air was heavy with moisture.

"It's sad to think you won't be in this house any more by tomorrow evening, Yumi," said Suga in a somber voice. Although she had known from the time of the first discussion of Yumi's marriage that sooner or later she would leave them, now that the time for parting was upon them Yumi acquired in her eyes the daring air of a young bird flapping its wings before flying away from the nest, and the futility of her own life, left alone in such a situation, was borne sharply home to her.

"There's nothing to be sad about. You've got so many people here—I'm sure *I* shall be the one to feel lonely, alone in a small house with just my elder sister."

Yumi spoke cheerfully as though to brighten her up, but Suga's eyes remained steadily fixed on Yumi's face, and she said as though speaking to herself:

"No, that kind of loneliness is different. When you go I shall be the one left alone in the background, here in this big house—that's what I mean. you're more positive than I am, Yumi."

"Positive?" demanded Yumi raising her head slightly. "Not me! The idea of me leaving here, you know—it was more than half because the master said I ought to settle down before I got too old. That makes it sound as though he's awfully concerned about me, but you know, Suga . . ." Disengaging her slender shoulder from the silk night kimono with an arrow-feather pattern, she brought her face close to Suga's, propping her chin on her elbow. "If the master really didn't want to let me go, do you think he'd say such a thing? Take us, now—with something we really valued, whether it was a kimono or an ornamental hairpin, we'd never sell it or give it away in a hurry, would we? I'm sure it's the same with men. Supposing you were in my place and asked to leave, he'd never let you. That's because it's you he's really fond of."

"No, it's not true. The one he's wrapped up in at the moment is the young mistress at Tsunamachi. Surely you know that."

Suga too had raised herself and turned to lie face down. Her voice shook as she mentioned Miya.

"That's true. But then, after all, legally she's the young master's wife. He may get some fun out of it but he can never have her openly in the eyes of society. The master himself is steadily getting older, and the mistress is more like the manager of the establishment. When it comes to looking after him personally, you're the only one he can't do without. *I'm* the one he doesn't need now that he's got the young mistress. I'm the 'fan in the autumn . . .' " She hummed a snatch of a *tokiwazu* melody and gave a light laugh. The slight self-mockery did not detract from the freshness of her laughter, but it failed to move Suga, who said in the same half-muttered tone:

"After all, the master's not young, is he? He seems to get tired when he goes to Tsunamachi. Preparing dried bonito broth, giving him five or six egg yolks to swallow at a time—that's the kind of extra work *I'm* likely to find myself with when you go. A servant cherished to death, that's me. When I look at it that way I envy you, clearing out definitely like this. If you marry Mr. Iwamoto you'll probably have children, and you'll be able to go out and about without feeling inferior to anybody."

"But on the other hand I shall miss not having to worry about money. You were only fifteen when you became part of the family here, so you know even less about the world than I do, but when I think of the hard times our family had at the worst period, I sometimes feel scared to leave. I'm . . . well, I suppose I'm used to accepting things, and I'm strong even though I'm not heavily built, so I can manage somehow, but *you* never could. The master always says you're like something fragile and breakable. He's right—you're all right wrapped up in your cocoon here, but one breath of the breeze outside and you'd be done for."

"I wouldn't mind so much, if only I could feel I *wanted* to leave here."

"You can't expect to. Not unless, say, there was someone you'd put up with any hardship for."

"But *you're* leaving even so, aren't you?"

"I'm different. I'm being got rid of, rather than leaving . . . Look at the Mr. Iwamoto I'm marrying—he's supposed to have a good head, but otherwise it's hardly a match anybody need envy, is it?"

"*I* envy you . . . I could die of envy."

As she spoke, Suga put her arms round the lacquered body of the wooden pillow and pressed her face down on it. The violence of the movement startled Yumi all the more in that it came from one who was normally so frustratingly indirect in her speech and unforthcoming in her manner.

Suga could find no way to express the feelings seething within her. If she put them into words they threatened to run wild in curses of an ugliness startling even to herself, or in rambling, ill-formulated complaints. It was something that Yumi could never be made to understand. She felt it as a predestined fate looming heavily over her whole life.

Why, long ago, had her parents not sold her to be a geisha instead of selling her to this family? As a geisha she would no doubt have been more exposed to the buffetings of the outside world, but at least she would have become more resilient as a person than she was now, and even though she might have had a patron she would have walked a little more freely in the sun, beneath the clear blue sky, have been a little more free to get angry and to weep.

She had enjoyed the love of a man old enough to be her father and a life of luxury beyond her station, yet as a man used to handling women Yukitomo had seen to it that even as he brought the young girl to the full flowering of womanhood she had always followed a course that did not clash with his keeping her in his own home, a course that she herself had docilely followed until she had become her present impotent self. Although Tomo seemed to mean nothing to Yukitomo where love was concerned, although in practice nothing about either of them conveyed any suggestion of marital affection, the patience and strength of will with which Tomo, unaided by her husband's love, maintained her position as mistress of the house gave Suga a sense of inadequacy that weighed on her day and night like an incredibly heavy stone.

Tomo's daily life held no ease or relaxation whatsoever. Deep down beneath the relaxed, gracious movements of her body there

120

lay concealed a constant, tense determination not to be outdone. Whatever outrages she might suffer at the hands of a husband with whom she had severed all ties of the flesh, she bore them unprotesting, with all the strength in her body. Knowing that anything she said to the women on whom Yukitomo bestowed his favors would produce an immediate and sensitive reaction in him, she never interfered with either Suga or Yumi. Yet precisely because of her silence, the close guard that she kept on every action in her own daily life acted as a strong though invisible check on Suga. And Yukitomo, who was well aware of this restraint that Tomo placed on Suga and the others, was quite content that it should be so.

There were times when Suga imagined how it would be if the mistress were to go away somewhere, but she was quite sure that no hints of her own could ever make Yukitomo turn her out. Sexually Tomo might mean nothing to Yukitomo, but she was secure in her position as his most trusted manager. He could have no more convenient and faithful supervisor of his affairs. Even supposing he got rid of Tomo, Suga would never have the ability to supervise the property; how much easier to go on living her days passive beneath the mistress' repressive regime than even to contemplate such a troublesome, disturbing idea ... But if the mistress were to die unavoidably and unexpectedly, it would be different. If such a thing happened, what a sense of relief it would bring, as though the thick layer of clouds lowering above her head had quite suddenly cleared away ... Each time she had such thoughts Suga felt guilty despite herself and strove to brush aside the cobwebs gathering about her heart. It was as though a devil had taken residence within her. At the same time, she felt quite clearly that she would never have been a devil had she not been trapped in her present surroundings.

Inside the self that achieved expression neither in action nor in words, that seemed so ineffectual, the feelings that could find no relief lay dark, cold, and silent, like snow settled by night.

The untroubled quality that Yumi maintained in the same situation had inspired Suga with envy as well as a sense of dissatisfaction, but now Yumi, with no resentment in her heart, was about to slip away out of the hell where Suga was helplessly floundering and fly up into the open skies ... In Suga's eyes Yumi was to be envied not for her marriage to Iwamoto but for her escape from the workings of the wheel of fate.

Suga knew, though, that Yumi would never understand this even if she were to tell her.

"Don't, Suga—don't cry, you'll make me sad too," said Yumi, shaking her by the shoulder. Suga lifted her face and saw Yumi's face close to hers and the tears brimming in the long, almond-shaped eyes. Yumi mistook my feeling, she thought, and was instantly seized with a burning shame; then in her eyes, too, the tears of sadness at parting with Yumi came welling up spontaneously.

"When you think about it, your destiny and mine must be linked somehow," said Yumi. "It's unusual for two women in the position of what people call concubines to look after the same master for a whole ten years and stay on good terms without quarreling. I think, you know ... perhaps we were sisters in a previous life?"

"I'm sure we were," said Suga in a voice full of emotion.

"In plays or in books the concubine's always a bad woman, isn't she? Giving the wife a hard time or causing trouble about inheritances and so on ... We've never done anything like that— we've been very good, I think, don't you?"

"The virtuous concubines ... But then, other people would never believe it if we told them."

"I don't care what other people think. Just the fact that we've been able to live like this for ten years is enough to prove to each other that we're not bad, isn't it?"

"You know, being loved by a man like the master—it's not that I dislike it, of course—but it can't help being different from falling really in love with someone around the same age as yourself, can it?"

At this point it occurred to Suga that she would never have been able to talk in this way before it was decided that Yumi should leave. And it occurred to her, too, that if Yumi became Iwamoto's wife and could come calling and be called on as an outsider to the family, she would have someone to talk to in a different way from hitherto. Suddenly she felt as though a bright window of light was shining into the closed confines of her heart.

"Yumi, have you noticed how the master lately has taken to talking about nothing but his health? I mean, what with bathing his eyes and gargling and so on, he may *look* well but he's getting on in years even so. You wait and see—before long he'll be just as indifferent to us as he is to the mistress."

"Yes, and with things the way they are at Tsunamachi, he wants to make himself look young again whenever he goes there. I really do think the young master's a strange kind of man. Whenever the master goes there he's always in such a good mood and gives him a lot of money to take himself out somewhere. Why, any normal person would surely sense something was up, but *he* doesn't have the remotest idea. I really feel sorry for him in a way, but . . . but he's not a normal man, is he?"

"Even so, he doesn't have any trouble in having children, does he?"

"Who's to say whose child it is? More like animals, I call it."

Yumi spoke with sharp contempt, but the immorality of it all did not trouble her so much as her words would suggest; the words did, however, trouble Suga.

"Oh no, the child's the young master's all right, or so they say. The master's long past having children, according to the mistress. I think so, too. I'm not strong, but you—when you marry Mr. Iwamoto, you'll be having children in no time."

"You may be right. But whether one can have children or not, what one does is the same isn't it?"

"Don't!" said Suga strenuously. "Don't tell me so clearly about something I can't do anything to change myself. *You* are going to leave here . . . but I've got stay here . . . always . . . I think you're inconsiderate!"

Her black eyes opened wide in resentment and she grasped Yumi's hand tightly in her own.

Some two months after returning to her parents' home, Yumi went to Iwamoto's home in Tamurachō as his bride.

It was an evening of steady drizzle in the rainy season, and it was after nine when Tomo came home by rickshaw from the reception to which she had been invited. At Tomo's greeting, Yukitomo, who was playing *go* with his doctor, looked round with a stone held between the tips of his long-jointed fingers.

"How was it? Did Yumi make a properly solemn bride?" he asked, and placed the stone on the board. He seemed to be winning and his voice was good-humored.

"She was a very well-bred looking bride—nothing fussy, an ordinary kimono with just a flower ornament in her hair," said Tomo in Suga's direction, and Yukitomo smiled and nodded. As she was making some vague answer to what Tomo had said, Suga gazed covertly at Yukitomo's profile, whose sunken temple showed how much he had aged recently; she was looking for some change of expression, but he was as unconcerned as though he were hearing about the marriage of a distant relative.

Iwamoto continued to come to the house on matters concern-

124

ing the land and houses, and each time Tomo and Suga would inquire after Yumi, whereupon he would wring his hands bashfully and reply with a little duck of his head:

"She's doing fine, thank you."

Miya, hearing on one of her visits how happy Iwamoto seemed to be, collapsed in frivolous giggles at the news.

"When Yumi's there alongside Mr. Iwamoto they must make a real beauty and the beast," she said. Then something apparently occurred to her, for she turned to Yukitomo and said, "Papa—why don't we go and have a look to see how the basketman's doing? You haven't been yet either, have you?" she added with a sideways glance at Suga.

Suga, who had been hoping to go and visit Yumi herself sometime and did not like the thought of the fuss involved in going with Miya and Yukitomo, made some vague reply, but Miya seemed much taken with her latest idea and went on in a wheedling tone:

"Really, Papa—why don't we? Let's go today if we're going. Yumi's place is in Tamurachō, so on the way back I'd like to go to the Ginza and look at hair ornaments."

"At Yumi's place they just weave baskets, that's all. There's nothing interesting to see. We don't want to interrupt them in their work."

"But what I mean is, we could just look in for a moment, couldn't we? Then we could go to the Ginza . . ."

"It makes me nervous, going to the Ginza with you," he said with a smile. Her playful way of talking and behaving, as if she were a young geisha making up to a man about town, showed a fine disregard for what people might think, and the more lively she became the more Suga's mood became heavy and funereal.

In the end Yukitomo set out that day, taking Miya and Suga with him. It was an invigorating autumn afternoon and a kite was piping shrilly from the clear blue sky.

Iwamoto's house stood in a sidestreet that led off to the left from the main street between Tamurachō and Shimbashi. In a neat, newly fitted room with a boarded floor stood a large number of new hampers painted with shiny black lacquer. Two youths were seated at work on the boards, weaving fine strips of bamboo and treating the paper stuck over the newly woven hampers with persimmon juice, preparatory to applying the lacquer.

Iwamoto had gone out to take an order. As the three of them alighted from their rickshaws Yumi came out, neat in a striped silk kimono with a mauve ribbon on her chignon, and took them into the best room at the back of the shop.

"You see, you have to be something of a skilled laborer in this business, and not being used to it I get tired," she said with a cheerful smile as she sat by the rectangular brazier making tea for them. "Where are you off to today?"

"We came out because Miya said she wanted to see your shop, but as you get older it takes a lot just to keep up with the young people ... Anyway, I'm glad you seem to be doing well."

"Thanks to you," said Yumi with a slight inclination of her head.

Yukitomo invited Yumi to come to the Ginza and have dinner with them, but she pleaded pressure of work in the shop; Yukitomo himself had been perfectly aware as he spoke that she would refuse, and after about an hour they left the shop, saying goodbye to Yumi at the entrance.

No sooner had they set off walking in the direction of Tsuchibashi than Miya said:

"Yumi's already like this, isn't she?" She made a curve with her hand over the region of her sash.

"What ...? Do you know, I never noticed!" said Suga, blinking her eyes as though dazzled by the light. It had occurred

126

to her, though, that all the while they had been in the house Yumi had kept on her yellow silk apron. The quickness of Miya's eye for such things struck her as indecent, as though it were somehow a sign of the lustful desires of her flesh, yet at the same time the suspicion that the child in Yumi's womb might be Yuki-tomo's brushed across her own mind, too, like the shadow of a passing bird. She knew that it could hardly be so in fact, but the idea gave her an odd pleasure, like that of pressing down hard on the root of an aching tooth. She felt like laughing at Michi-masa and the other husband, Iwamoto—laughing with the utterly cold and beautiful laugh of the harpy who rips open the bellies of pregnant women . . .

Yukitomo was walking ahead briskly using his stick, deaf apparently to the women's talk. Seen from the front, he seemed to have aged strikingly, but his step was youthful and his back as stiff as a ramrod.

In midsummer the following year Yumi came to the Shirakawas' carrying her new baby.

Miya too was there at the big house that day with her own child. Kazuyo, Miya's child, was two years younger than Takao and just one year older than Yumi's firstborn, Naoichi.

When she saw Naoichi's face, so smooth and well-formed, Miya's eyes narrowed in a smile.

"Naoichi's so good-looking!" she said as she played with him. "I'm sure he'll have all the ladies after him when he grows up." Her soft, melting smile as she said this was so completely artless that even the wary Tomo was obliged to smile.

While keeping an eye on Takao, who was running about nearby with his nurse in attendance, Tomo gazed at the children in Miya's and Yumi's arms, both of them boys, with something akin to wonder.

127

Takao, Kazuya, Naoichi . . . Eventually they too, she supposed, would grow up into adult men. Even now the idea still came as a kind of shock. It was a disturbing sensation quite different from the feeling when she imagined the figure that Takao would cut on the day he came of age. It disturbed her to think that these small creatures now innocently romping in front of her, laughing and making faces, would one day become men just like any others: men like Yukitomo, like Michimasa, like Iwamoto . . .

It occurred to Tomo that among the women there was one who sat with no child: Suga. Her lap, strangely empty, told of her loneliness far more eloquently than her face could ever do.

"I wonder if Suga isn't envious because Yumi's got married? I wouldn't mind marrying her off if there was a suitable match . . ." The remark made by Yukitomo two or three days previously as he was showing Takao the carp in the pond still lodged heavy in Tomo's breast. Nowadays Suga would often, even when others were present, have a vacant look in her eyes as though gazing into space. Frequently Tomo noticed that her eyes were swollen at the rims as though she had been crying in the privacy of her room. The cause, Tomo surmised, was twofold: loneliness at having lost Yumi, and the pain of watching Miya happily basking in Yukitomo's love. Could it be that Yukitomo was growing weary of the resistance in Suga that found no expression in words but seemed to seep from her body?

"But Suga's different from Yumi," she had said. "Her periods aren't normal, and even if she got married she probably couldn't have children. For myself too, I'd prefer it that she should always be here to look after you . . ." Tomo had got so far and broken off in a sweat, fearful lest the criticism of Yukitomo implied in her words should strike home. But Yukitomo had merely nodded equivocally and without replying had clapped his hands above the water.

"Look," he said, tapping Takao on the shoulder. "Here come the carp! Here they come!"

Tomo felt an overwhelming pity for Suga, the woman whom Yukitomo no longer needed. Yumi and Miya were different: even though she were abandoned by Yukitomo, Yumi had a new husband and could bear children, while Miya was the kind of woman who could probably make any man go on loving her indefinitely without wearying of her charms.

Suga had become Yukitomo's mistress before she had even started menstruating, and this almost certainly was what had damaged her ability to bear children. Now that she was over thirty and beginning to lose her good looks she could hardly become a geisha, nor if she married was it likely, with her sickly constitution, that things would go as smoothly as with Yumi. At the thought of the ultimate fate awaiting Suga—to grow gradually older while leading the concubine's life that she loathed, sharing with a woman whose presence made her uneasy the care of one man, Yukitomo—gloom would settle over her irresistibly. There was no use in expressing the sympathy she felt, for Suga would only interpret her words cynically as concern for herself.

Tomo was aware of the accusation in Suga's baleful gaze, which seemed to say, "It is you who brought me to this fate." It afforded her a wry amusement, too, to note that Suga's resentment toward Yukitomo was not so strong as toward herself.

As she watched the three small boys, a sudden wave of abhorrence made her suddenly turn back to Suga's childless lap with something like a sense of relief. "What do you want with children?" she longed to whisper to Suga. "They only tie you more tightly to the wheel of fate."

Unripe Damsons

Halfway down the west-facing slope of the elevation on which the house stood there was a flat stretch of land overgrown with tall weeds. When Yukitomo, shortly after the end of the Sino-Japanese war, had first bought and moved into what had once been a foreigner's residence he had planted on this piece of vacant land a large number of young plums, peaches, loquats, almonds, persimmons and other trees, since fruit-bearing trees gave the grounds, he said, a more lively air. By now, more than a dozen years later, they had grown to a considerable size and the spot made an ideal playground for the steadily growing band of grandchildren, who would spend their time climbing the trees or helping themselves to the fruit.

Yukitomo's father, a low-ranking samurai of the Hosokawa clan, had been in charge of the waxtree farms, and even as a small child Yukitomo had been intrigued by the orchards that yielded the raw material for making the wax on which part of the clan's finances depended. It was this perhaps that had made him fond of all trees, and especially trees that bore fruit, which were inseparably associated in his mind with wealth. During the time when he had worked at the Fukushima prefectural office, he had turned the land at the back of his official residence into an orchard in which he planted newly imported Western varieties of cherry and apple, obtained from the agricultural research station of the prefecture, and would watch in wonder as the great cherries and bright red apples ripened. Even now that he was past sixty it gave him exquisite pleasure to live in a house with nearly two acres of grounds and to savor the fruit off his own land.

Most numerous among the trees were damsons, whose fruit was not allowed to turn ripe and yellow but was shaken down and pickled in tubs while still green. The pickled damsons were carefully put in jars and labeled each year. The relatives all got their share, but still there were old jars left whose contents grew more mature every year, the damsons softer with a special, tart sweetness. Every morning without fail one of them appeared on Yukitomo's breakfast table for the sake of his health.

One fine day when the May rains had let up temporarily, it was decided to shake down the plums.

It was a Saturday and Takao, now at primary school, together with his younger halfbrothers Kazuya and Tomoya, were dashing about in the shifting flecks of sunlight that fell through the green leaves, helping Suga and the maids to shake the trees or carrying baskets for the fruit.

Standing in the fork of the largest tree of all could be seen the thin legs of a young man whose face was hidden among the foliage.

"Mr. Konno—isn't that all yet? This tree has an awful lot of fruit, doesn't it!" called Suga, in her voluminous indigo-striped flannel kimono, as she peered up into the swaying branches. A thin face with silver-framed spectacles peered out through the leaves and thin lips parted in a smile to reveal white teeth.

"No, not yet. I can get at least two or three pounds more."

"I should think that's about enough, isn't it? We must have got nearly thirty pounds already. We can't eat pickled damsons all the year round."

"Konno—come on down! Let's go and play ball on the front lawn!"

"Yes, I'm fed up with plum picking, Mr. Konno. Come on down, now!"

There was a difference in the way the two grandchildren of the family—Takao the eldest son, brought up at the big house by his grandparents, and Kazuya who lived in his parents' smaller house—addressed the houseboy.

Deaf to their pleas, Konno stayed where he was in the fork of the tree.

"I'll be down in a minute. Why don't you boys go ahead? If I don't get them all down your grandmother will be cross," he said and went on shaking the branches busily.

For a while Takao and his companions continued to set up a clamor, but before long they called, "You come later then—we'll be on the lawn," and ran off gleefully up the slope.

"It's really all right, though, Mr. Konno. Don't bother any more, now—come down and have a rest. Look, you said you have to get down to work for your exams today, didn't you?"

"Yes, but they don't start till six."

"Even so, when you have an exam you ought to settle down and look at your books a bit first."

"I'm all right," he said with a laugh and clambered down out of the tree, placing one foot after the other on knots in the branches then leaping lightly down the last few feet.

"Nobu and Yoshi, take these to the kitchen and wash them, will you?" Suga ordered the maids, who raised the basket with great apparent effort and set off with bowed backs up the slope.

"Look what a lot of leaves you shook off! They give off such a leafy smell," she said, taking up the broom and setting about sweeping together the scattered foliage.

"I'll do that, Mrs. Shirakawa."

"No, you have a rest."

"Don't be silly. It's only a day or two since you were in bed with a headache, isn't it? You don't want to make yourself giddy, do you?" He wrested the broom from Suga's hand and briskly began to sweep.

For a while Suga's eyes were fixed on the ground, from which arose a scent of grass stirred up by Konno's energetic movements with the broom, then she said without looking up:

"You mustn't call me Mrs. Shirakawa again, Mr. Konno."

"Oh lord!" muttered Konno to himself and stopped wielding the broom. "I'm sorry—really. I must have got into the habit. Even so, there's nobody around, so it doesn't matter, does it?"

"Even if there's not, you'll soon hear about it from somebody. It makes it difficult for me."

"I suppose I shall be told again that there aren't two mistresses in this house. Someone said she was just like the Empress of China. Unpleasant old woman, isn't she?"

" 'Old woman'! Really, Mr. Konno, to call the mistress of the house . . .!"

"There's only one head of this house, and that's the master. I hate hearing that old woman talking to you as if you were a maid. They keep on calling her the 'mistress,' but nowadays she has nothing to do with the master, does she? Surely it's you who's the real mistress?"

Suga stood with one hand on the plum tree, her white toes idly playing with her garden clog as she listened to Konno's protestations. The words uttered by the young pharmacology student affected her mind with a pleasurable pain.

"You shouldn't say such things. The mistress is a great deal more strong-willed underneath than the master. However things may look, he's got a healthy respect for her. You won't stay in this house long, either, if she takes a dislike to you."

"Fat lot I care!" With a sulky look Konno flung aside the broom with which he had just finished the sweeping.

"You're too docile, Suga. You ought to have a word in the master's ear and get him to put that old woman in her place."

"What an idea—as if I could!" muttered Suga, opening wide her great, gloomy eyes in which pale blue specks were visible.

Two or three days previously, Tomo had sent Konno to the local ward office for some papers which, as she was out when he returned, he had given to Suga instead of handing them to her personally. Later, Tomo had called to Konno as he was walking along the corridor.

"Mr. Konno—did you do what I asked at the ward office?"

"Yes, I brought the papers but you were out, so I gave them to the mistress."

Konno, who habitually went rather tense when spoken to by Tomo, hunched his shoulders together deferentially and spoke formally, as usual.

"I see . . . so you gave them to Suga."

"Yes, ma'am." He was about to move off when Tomo pulled him up with a slight cough.

"Er, Mr. Konno—there's something I'd like to remind you of. You will please not refer to Suga as the mistress. There is only one mistress in this house—myself. If one is loose in one's speech, you see, the whole household tends to get out of hand."

Her tone was mild, but the effect on Konno was like a sudden hammer-blow to the head. Bowing obsequiously, he glanced at her out of the corner of his eye as he made off, only to find her smooth, sallow cheeks as calm and relaxed as ever, the same, faintly drowsy fullness in her eyelids.

A year or so earlier, when he had come as houseboy to the Shirakawas, on the understanding that they would give him the time and money needed to attend night classes at a pharmacological college, Konno had referred to Suga as "Miss Suga" in the same way as the maids and tradesmen. It somehow suggested a housekeeper, and it was Suga indeed who, when Tomo, as so often happened, was out attending to their land and houses, moved lethargically back and forth between living quarters and kitchen, taking care of Yukitomo's needs and giving instructions for the running of the household. When she had nothing on her hands she would sit by the rectangular brazier in the living room smoking her long-stemmed pipe or reading aloud from a book or newspaper to keep Yukitomo amused. At night, of course, she set her bed out beside Yukitomo's in his bedroom; but apart from this the thing that most clearly showed Suga's position in the Shirakawa household was the seating arrangement of the members at mealtimes.

Yukitomo would sit in the most honored position, followed by Tomo and Takao, with Michimasa, his wife Miya, and their children in the appropriate places whenever they happened to be there. Then small lacquered tables would be brought and placed before each of them, while the serving maid placed a large lacquered tub containing cooked rice in the center of the room and seated herself before it. No separate table was set out for Suga. With her back to the maid, she would sit facing Yukitomo across his table, helping him to rice, boning his fish, and otherwise attending to his needs while she herself ate from dishes placed on the same table.

The sight of the elderly Yukitomo plying his chopsticks with the younger Suga seated opposite him at the same table suggested a relationship whose familiarity was neither that of husband and wife nor that of father and daughter, and confirmed Suga's position at a glance to anyone who might be watching.

To Konno, too, the sight gradually elucidated the peculiar nuance with which the maids and tradespeople referred to her as "Miss Suga." Born the third in a family of nine and sent to work for a while in an ordinary pharmacy in Chiba after he left middle school, Konno had conceived the ambition of obtaining a pharmacologist's license and had come to Tokyo, where he had already foisted himself on two or three different families. In his admittedly shallow way he was swift to detect where the authority lay in a household, which strings when pulled would move which limbs, and he knew well how to worm his way into the subtle gaps offered by a complex set of domestic relationships. As he began to make himself at home he soon divined that Yukitomo was the absolute authority in the Shirakawa household, that Tomo was in the position of a manager with few close ties with her husband, and that Suga and the grandson Takao were the true objects of Yukitomo's affection.

Takao could do no wrong in either Yukitomo's or Tomo's eyes. Suga too, in compliance with Yukitomo's wishes, looked after him almost as a nurse, so one sure tactic was to play up to "Master Takao." More important still, though, a young man such as Konno with no relations at hand must look to the maids every time his clothes even needed mending, and here the quickest method was to get Tomo or Suga to speak to them for him.

Tomo with her quiet, ever watchful manner had an inscrutability that kept Konno at a distance no matter how long he knew her, but behind Suga's slowness of speech and the lethargy of her movements he glimpsed a great, gray shadow that spoke eloquently of aspirations unfulfilled in this household.

"I wonder why Miss Suga doesn't leave here and get him to set her up in her own house?" he said one day to Maki, Takao's nurse. "If she did that, she might still be a concubine, but at least she'd be mistress in her own home to do as she pleased." But Maki shook her head and said:

"She doesn't have it in her. Not for all her inward, sulky . . . After all, she came into service here when she was fifteen, and she's been in this house for nearly twenty years. How could you expect

136

her to know how to get round the master? Besides, the master's always been a man who liked his own way, and he'd be sure to object to letting a woman go once she was his own property. All the more so nowadays, now that he's getting on in years. Poor Miss Suga, I feel sorry for her when I think of the future, her with no children or anything."

It was shortly after hearing this explanation that Konno took to calling Suga "Mrs. Shirakawa" and referring to her before others as "the young mistress."

The first time he used it casually to her Suga seemed startled. Opening her eyes wide, she parted her lips as though about to correct him, but in the end she swallowed hard and let it pass. Even so, the joy that had flickered like lightning across her tense features had not escaped Konno.

"Mr. Konno, the master says he doesn't like to see your blue cotton kimono, it's so faded. So I bought this roll of dyed cotton. I'll have Yoshi make it up—why don't you wear it instead?"

As she showed him the material her voice sounded dispirited, for all the world as though she were acting unwillingly at Yukitomo's command. In fact, it was she who had put the idea into Yukitomo's mind.

"Mr. Konno's always taking Master Takao out, but he looks disgraceful, I think, in that dyed cotton kimono all out at the elbows. And it isn't as if one can keep complaining at someone who's only a houseboy, is it?" she had said casually with a frown, and Yukitomo had reprimanded her:

"What are you thinking of, woman? Why don't you do what you think fit to make sure he looks all right? He's a member of the household, isn't he? You ought to think more of our reputation."

Though Konno might call her "the mistress," it did not mean that the maids and tradespeople would also change their way of referring to her. She knew too that if they should do so she herself would be obliged to correct them.

Nevertheless, the words "the mistress" as spoken by Konno titillated her ears with an indescribable pleasure.

However she might be cherished in private, Suga could never be really free and open, never feel the bright sun's rays upon her so long as she lived under the same roof as Yukitomo's legal wife. She must lurk forever in the background behind Tomo, waiting with watchful eyes and neck craned greedily forward.

Not even Yukitomo, much less Tomo, had any idea of the hopeless frustration and impotence that she felt. And since it was so, Konno's ill-considered words of flattery wormed their way insidiously into her heart.

Once Suga began to show herself favorably disposed, Konno began to whisper unconcealed slander of Tomo in her ear.

The more heated Konno became in attacking Tomo, the more Suga retreated into her defense. The more she defended her, the more she enjoyed the picture of herself as a decent woman so unlike the usual run of mistresses; but she failed to notice how, as they pulled first one way then the other like the two sides in a tug-o'-war, the distance between herself and Konno grew steadily narrower.

As one who while still a girl had been loved by a man thirty years her senior, who had continued to coddle her ever since, Suga was too irrevocably the child-woman to feel motherly love for a man her junior by ten years. To eyes familiar with Yukitomo, Konno as a man was hopelessly lightweight, lacking completely in the more dignified masculine qualities. At first, indeed, she had thought so little of him that it would probably never have occurred to her even to make such a comparison, yet as he began to show his malice towards Tomo both his face and his body, shallow and insubstantial though they were, began to produce a strong though different impact on her.

Konno knew that Suga suffered from chronic hemorrhoids that caused her pain and fever, an affliction all the more distressing because she would not tell others of her trouble. So, being friendly with the pharmocologist in a drugstore, he would bring some Chinese herbal infusion that she had never heard of and give it to her when no one was about. Whenever she tried to pay for it, he would push the money away from him with the fingers of his pallid hand spread wide as he walked away.

"It's all right, it's all right," he would say. "What's more important is that Her Highness will make a fuss if she hears, so don't tell anyone you're taking it."

In anyone else such behavior, with its suggestion that she was not properly loved by her protector Yukitomo, would have aroused Suga's indignation, but the medicine that Konno gave her was carefully transferred to a can and duly infused and drunk as though it were something very precious.

"That's an odd-smelling medicine—are you sure it's not the stuff they put in the bathwater?" Yukitomo would ask at times half-teasingly, but she would smile blankly and reply:

"My sister-in-law sent it from home. It's good for my usual trouble," she said. "I wonder what it's called?" The melancholy ghost of a smile that rose to one side of her face at such times had an almost uncanny air of coquetry; it was the closest she would ever get to avenging herself on Yukitomo.

In the other house, Miya was presenting her husband with another child almost every year, though there was no guarantee that among the five there was no offspring of Yukitomo's. Michimasa in his near imbecility never dreamed of the true relationship between his father and his wife, but the mere necessity of guarding the secret had earned him during the past few years a kind of

139

generosity from his father that he had never known before. By now the house at Tsunamachi was for Yukitomo not so much his son's home as a secret love nest.

Suga would feel a familiar, wry amusement at the clearly renewed sexual ardor of Yukitomo's gaze during the periods between the first morning sickness that sent Miya to her bed and her recovery following the birth of the child.

Try as she might to convince herself that all men were alike, the same frustrating sense of groping through some endless darkness stayed with her forever, shriveling her heart with a dull pain. So it was that the inner mechanism that should automatically have rebuffed Konno, for whom she had no particular fancy, failed to work with its full efficiency.

"Oh . . . !" Standing there in the green sunlight Suga suddenly hunched her shoulders and wriggled her neck to and fro.

"What is it?" said Konno coming up, startled by her cry.

"I'm not sure. I think it's something down my back. Oh! It's moving! Mr. Konno—have a look for me, will you?"

"What is it? Have you got an insect or something down there?"

"Oh! It's horrid! It tickles!"

"Here, excuse me a moment."

As he spoke he put his hand down between Suga's kimono and her plump white back.

"Let's see. Where—here?"

"No—the other way. It's stinging me! Yes—about there."

"Well!—it's only a caterpillar!"

"How horrid!"

Hardly knowing what she was doing, Suga wriggled free of Konno's hand and gave a shudder. Konno laughed as he squashed with his wooden clog the small damson-tree caterpillar that he had thrown at their feet.

140

"You've gone quite pale. Coward! All because of a caterpillar!"

"But they're horrid. Don't you know the saying, 'to detest someone like a caterpillar'?"

Suga put both hands up to her neck and busily brushed up the loose hairs from her bushy chignon as though afraid she still had a caterpillar crawling on her neck. More than the unhealthy beauty of her face, with the eyes in which specks were to be seen around the rim, it was the cool clamminess of the fair skin his hand had just touched that made Konno's whole being shudder with an unnatural sensuous excitement.

"It still prickles. I wonder if it stung me?"

"Let's have a look."

He made to approach her back again but Suga straightened her clothes. "It's all right, I'll go and get Yoshi to have a look and put some medicine on," she said, and set off at a brisk pace.

Seated together with some forty or fifty others in the hall of the annex to the Nishi Honganji temple in Tsukiji, Tomo was listening avidly to each word of the lecture being delivered from the dais. The speaker, a scholar-priest sent from the headquarters of the sect in Kyoto, had a close-cropped head, a grim expression, and thick-lensed spectacles before his short-sighted eyes, and he wore a narrow surplice over his summer jacket of black silk gauze.

The subject of the lecture was the story of the Lady Vaidehi, the first person to whom the Buddha taught the Pure Land faith and an indispensable figure in the teachings of the Shin Sect of Pure Land Buddhism.

According to Buddhist legend, The Lady Vaidehi and her spouse the King Bimbisara had no issue. The king prayed to the gods and buddhas that they might be blessed with children, and as a result they were told that the holy man who had transmitted the divine word was to be reborn as a prince, but that this could

141

only take place after the ascetic's death. The king waited impatiently for the ascetic's death, but many years passed with no sign of the longed-for event. Finally, unable to wait any longer in his compelling desire for a son, the king, unbeknown to his wife, ordered a retainer to murder the ascetic, whereupon the Lady Vaidehi immediately conceived and in due course brought forth an infant prince.

Greatly rejoicing, the king dearly cherished the prince whom he named Ajatasatru, but from an early age Ajatasatru showed a violent disposition. He treated his father as an enemy, and as he grew older his savage strength went more and more unchecked, until finally he imprisoned the king his father and set about starving him to death.

Great as the king's suffering was, it was as nothing compared to that of the Lady Vaidehi, forced to watch helplessly as her son cruelly sought to do his own father to death. A royal consort and mother to a powerful despot, she lacked almost nothing in human rank and riches, yet her heart day and night suffered constant torments, and she called on heaven and earth in her anguish to witness the strange injustice that the child of her own womb should resemble her so little.

Hoping to keep her husband alive, she would smear honey over her body and, stealing by night into the cave that was his prison, let him lick her skin as he lay, wasted by disease, in the darkness. In this way she kept him barely alive for a while, but eventually she was discovered by Ajase and herself thrown into confinement in one of the remotest dungeons of the palace.

Cut off from all action that might alleviate the evil that her son committed, the Lady Vaidehi was left helplessly to bewail her own powerlessness.

The Lady Vaidehi at that time was indeed sunk deep in hell, a world of boundless darkness and horror where all harmony and all reason lay crushed to dust. As she strained her eyes to see into the invisible world at the bottom of the dark pit, still the Lady Vaidehi went on praying with the little strength still left in her helpless body. She longed for the light; and earnestly, passionately, she began to call on the Lord Buddha in his far distant realm:

"Lord Buddha, Lord Buddha! Grant strength to this helpless life. Why must I struggle to go on living in this ugly, deformed world of men?"

The prayer reached the ears of the Buddha, who transported himself across many hundreds of leagues to appear in all his radiant glory before the Lady Vaidehi in her prison.

He explained to her, as she lay half dead with suffering, the workings of fate attendant on the birth of Ajatasatru, and described to her the resplendent glories of the Pure Land that would eventually open up before her who, though bound fast by karma, so devoutly maintained the faith. The Buddha's teachings to her constitute what is known today as the *Amitayur-dhyana Sutra*.

The sufferings of the Lady Vaidehi were a part of the cruel karma that men, for all their wisdom and power, can do nothing to assuage. With a heart both intelligent and compassionate, she carried in her womb an evil soul, the product of her husband's karma, and was unable to escape the tortures of the devil to which she had given birth. The easiest way would have been to become like Ajatasatru. Yet to be an Ajatasatru was eternally impossible for her, while not to join forces with him was to be condemned eternally to a spiritual hell.

"The Lady Vaidehi realized," said the lecturer, "that authority, material wealth, wisdom—all things in which men put their trust—were powerless and impermanent, and the realization made her so eager to be delivered from such a hell that she cried out to Shakyamuni. She called on the Buddha in the name of all ordinary women who are cut off entirely from attaining the faith through their own powers. The Buddha answered her desperate cry, and administered to her the teaching of salvation through reliance. That famous passage in the work of our founder, Saint Shinran— 'Even the virtuous man attains rebirth in Paradise: how much more so, then, the sinner?'—is an exposition of this type of salvation. A man may believe himself just, yet if he opens his eyes a little wider he will see that he is affected by all kinds of karma and that all unawares he is creating boundless evil. He can do nothing about this through his own powers; only the light from without, the grace of the Lord Amida, can bring him salvation. It is our sect's belief that this grace is embodied in the invocation of his holy name: *Namu Amida Butsu.*"

The lecturer gave two or three more examples of the type of reliance on divine aid shown by the Lady Vaidehi, then left the platform.

Among the assembled women there were some who, even during the lecture, were continually murmuring "*Namu Amida Butsu, Namu Amida Butsu . . .*" After the lecturer had gone, tea and cakes were served to each of them, which they took up reverently as they began to talk amongst themselves not so much of the sermon they had just heard as of the doings of each other's families. An organization of believers known as the "Ladies' Church" and consisting mostly of women of the middle class or above, they invariably included a sermon by a visiting lecturer in their regular monthly meeting. Sometimes someone would bring an unmarried daughter or a young woman, but most of them were middle-aged or elderly women of the well-to-do classes; occasionally, even, a celebrated bluestocking, sister to the chief abbot of the temple, was to be seen among them, conspicuous as she sat absolutely upright with her long neck like a crane's.

Tomo exchanged a few words on everyday subjects with some

businessmen's wives of her acquaintance, took up her familiar hold-all and left the meeting somewhat before the rest of them. She had to call at an agent's house about raising the land rent on their estate at Kodemmachō.

Devoutly pressing her palms together in front of her breast as she passed before the main hall of the temple, she made her way out of the temple's spacious grounds and set off in the direction of Shintomichō, her mind dwelling as she went on the religious faith shown by the Lady Vaidehi.

Tomo's first acquaintance with the teachings of the Shin sect of Buddhism had come about at the wish of her mother, now long since dead.

A few years before her mother's death at her elder brother's house in Kumamoto, a dozen or more years previously, Tomo had yielded to her wishes and traveled all the way to Kyushu to see her, taking with her the then still youthful Suga.

She had wanted to calm the fears that her mother felt at hearing that Suga had come to be Yukitomo's mistress, to calm them by letting her see with her own eyes that this concubine was not a woman to be dreaded but a gentle girl more like a young bride.

Her mother indeed had seemed even more reassured than Tomo had expected, yet nonetheless it seemed to make her appreciate still more keenly the heaviness of Tomo's heart at the idea of such a young and beautiful woman living under the same roof and serving Yukitomo throughout the long years to come.

"However much we fret, we mortals can't arrange things to suit ourselves. You should take that to heart and never force things but leave everything to the Lord Amida," she had said, and again and again she had advised Tomo to attend the Hongan-ji temple on her return to Tokyo, so as to avail herself of the comforts of the Shin faith.

But it was not until after her mother's death that Tomo had

put her advice into practice. Even though she had not fulfilled her promise during her mother's lifetime, she had always had the excuse that household affairs did not allow her sufficient leisure, but once a husband had been found for Etsuko, and a wife, however unsatisfactory, for Michimasa, of whose marriage she had almost despaired, the last wishes of her departed mother had come to seem like a duty that she could not decently ignore.

Nonetheless, for some time it was no more than a feeling of duty to her mother that took her to worship or to hear the priests' lectures, for the constant painful efforts she must make to cover up for Yukitomo's loose behavior and ensure that it did not undermine the foundations of the family seemed unlikely to be assuaged by abstract phrases such as "the vow of the Lord Amida."

It was not until around the time when she first learned of the illicit relationship between her daughter-in-law Miya and Yukitomo that the first small buds of faith began to form in her mind.

No one could tell the sorrow and loathing aroused in Tomo through the years by Michimasa's excessively self-centered, almost half-witted nature. However despotic a husband Yukitomo might be, he had quite enough sense to realize that his own position depended on others and on society at large; in that sense, at least, he was to be respected as a man. But in Michimasa's mind neither the code of conduct nor the love that had served as Tomo's creed throughout her life carried any weight whatsoever. Just as in dealing with others he always ended by offending them, so towards the woman he had taken as his wife Michimasa felt no love of any kind other than the desire that was satisfied by the flesh. It was doubtful even whether Miya would have stayed so long with Michimasa had she not known that the same house harbored the unexpected happiness yielded by Yukitomo's skillful attentions.

At the period when she had first heard about Miya, Tomo's

samurai breeding had made her violently scorn Miya's delight in being trifled with by her father-in-law; Miya was a wretched woman, rotten to the core. Used though Tomo was to the constant sense of gloom and vague dissatisfaction caused by Yukitomo's relations with women even apart from Suga and Yumi, she could not help feeling a fresh alarm when faced with the question of Miya.

If Michimasa should get wind of what was happening and his half-imbecile mind be provoked into actual violence, the reputation of the Shirakawa family that she had always hugged so jealously to herself might be reduced to ruins. By now she was less concerned with her own fate, caught beneath the debris, than with the possible injury to Takao, whom she had reared so lovingly beneath her wing.

She herself had never foreseen that she would come to lavish so much affection on her grandchild. The pity she felt for an infant that had lost its mother at birth had transformed itself into love. It mattered not the slightest that the child was the son of the stupid, abrasive Michimasa; the blood tie only made Takao seem all the more pathetic and lovable. How cold, how unbending she had been in rearing her own children, Michimasa and Etsuko, in comparison with the love that welled up so abundantly and so blindly for this child!

Set in the scales of the love she felt for Takao, Tomo felt a fresh responsibility not only for Michimasa but for Miya and Suga as well. Both Suga, the flower plucked by Yukitomo while still in the bud, and Miya, whose frustration with her loutish husband had been taken advantage of by her father-in-law, came to seem more to be pitied than hated. And when she reflected that the men in question were the husband and son to whom she was bound by inseparable ties, she felt herself powerless in the coils of a cycle of birth and rebirth that reminded her vividly of the hell

147

into which the Lady Vaidehi had been cast; thus for the first time the invocation to Amida rose quite naturally and effortlessly to her lips. The depth of her love for Takao and the dark sense of revulsion against her own complicity in the four-way relationship of husband, son, mistress and daughter-in-law were burdens almost too heavy for Tomo to bear, yet she had entered into neither of them of her own free will, any more than she could voluntarily escape from their hold.

Of late, Tomo was beset by yet another anxiety. It was something that she had heard while she was at Tsunamachi one day, when Miya, who was growing visibly plumper, had remarked cheerfully as she placed a glossy nipple in the mouth of her fifth child Namiko:

"Mother, they say that Miss Suga's going to get married . . . Did you know?"

"Of course she's not. Who told you such a thing?"

Her voice was casual as she knocked out her short pipe on the brazier, but something inside her gave a sudden lurch.

"Father says so. 'Suga seems to have taken a fancy to that young Konno,' he said. 'Their ages are a bit different, but when he leaves college I'm thinking of getting them married and setting them up with their own chemist's shop . . .' "

"Well! Fancy his saying a thing like that! I imagine he was joking. Just think of it—after all, Konno and Suga are nearly ten years different in age."

She gave a little forced laugh, and Miya collapsed in mirth, screwing her eyes up into narrow creases as though she found the idea irresistibly funny.

"But you know, that's not really the point in this kind of case," she said. "What does it matter so long as they're fond of each other . . .? Even so, I suppose it would be hard for Father himself, if he lost Suga after all this time."

Miya spoke as though the whole matter was remote from herself, blithely disregarding her own secret.

"It certainly would be hard! For me, if not for Father. By now it's too late to have another woman in the house, and . . . No, I'm sure that Suga herself, even though she takes his part a lot, isn't mixed up with Konno in any way," Tomo concluded firmly, and took her leave, but from then on she began to watch anxiously for signs of intimacy between Suga and Konno.

In the long years that she had been plagued by Yukitomo's ways with women Tomo had naturally acquired the intuitive ability to detect the presence or otherwise of physical relations between a man and woman. Even when she was with many other people she could tell by some sixth sense, through the exchange of private glances, if a relationship was other than regular. And so far as she could judge by that instinctive sense, no such secret had as yet developed between Suga and Konno.

The one thing that had changed of late was that Suga obviously took Konno's part, yet she seemed to show no awkwardness towards Yukitomo, who actually seemed to take pleasure in the growing intimacy between her and the young man.

Only the other day a letter from Konno's parents saying that they wished to come to see the sights of Tokyo had been passed on to Suga by Konno and by Suga to Yukitomo, who had immediately proposed that they be invited to stay at the Shirakawa residence.

Konno refused vehemently. "They're only country folk, and I'd be embarrassed if the maids made fun of them . . ." But Yukitomo insisted almost angrily that he invite them.

"If they're going to do the sights of Tokyo, you should go with them too, Suga," he said. "If Konno went by himself when he was supposed to be working, his parents would probably feel awkward."

149

He took a considerable sum of money out of a stationery box and handed it to her. Suga herself had looked unusually animated.

"Yes, that's a good idea—since they've come all this way, they ought to have some memories to take back with them besides the usual tower at Asakusa and the Imperial Palace. It's not long before the summer fireworks display on the Sumida, so while I'm about it shall I take them to the Kusumi's on that day so that they can see them?"

Tomo reflected wryly that it was hardly necessary to go to quite so much trouble for the houseboy's parents but she stayed silent, knowing that to speak up at such times would only make her husband despise her all the more as an interfering busybody.

They took them to see not only the fireworks but the Bon dancing as well, and even out of town as far as Enoshima and Kamakura, on which occasions Suga went with them for all the world as though she really intended to become Konno's wife, with her hair done up in a youthful chignon with the front generously fluffed up, dressed in a thin summer kimono of Akashi crepe with a vertical stripe that showed off to perfection the fair complexion of which she was so proud. Far from being put out by all this, Yukitomo would ask them all kinds of questions about their day when they returned, taking pleasure in the wonder shown by Konno's folks from the country. It was very different from the days when Suga was younger, when he would show his displeasure if she so much as spoke to another man. Could it be that he had reached an age to take pleasure in seeing her on friendly terms with a man so young and ineffectual? Or could it be that now that he had Miya he hoped to pass Suga off on Konno?

Close to them though she was, Tomo could tell neither Yukitomo's nor Suga's true feelings.

150

She toyed with the idea of an indirect warning to Suga, but even if Suga had not been oddly excited lately, the very mention of Konno would have been enough to put her visibly on her guard, so Tomo decided to let well enough alone and remain a passive observer.

Could it be that in her late thirties a belated love was at last putting forth buds in Suga? Even should it be so, if she were really infatuated with someone like Konno, a man with no true ability, lacking both judgment and firmness of character, she was certainly heading for unhappiness. Tomo's own nature made it painfully impossible for her to dismiss the affair as Suga's own foolishness. At such times, she could forget nothing, not even how when she had first gone to fetch Suga she had been asked by Suga's mother, now dead, to look after her daughter's future welfare.

One day after Suga had gone out shopping Tomo summoned Konno and as casually as possible asked him if he was intending to marry Suga.

"Good heavens, no. Miss Suga's ten years older than me for one thing, and besides, she's not strong enough to be an ordinary wife. Marriage for me means children and grandchildren; I don't want any barren woman, thank you," he said, his lips quivering with a shallow smile. His main concern, his tone suggested, was lest he should mistakenly be thought to have been making advances to Suga.

"I see . . . That's all right then. You've got to think about your own future, you see, and if there were anything between you and Suga we should have to take steps to end it, which wouldn't be pleasant for either of you. The master may look very easy-going but he deals with that kind of thing in no uncertain way . . ."

She looked Konno straight in the eyes as she spoke, with no

151

hint of what she had heard from Miya concerning Yukitomo's private intentions. Perceiving that Konno was not in love with Suga she had tried a high-handed approach and, as she expected, Konno's pallid face with its silver-rimmed spectacles had shown irresolution, then begun to cringe unpleasantly as she watched.

From then on Konno's manner towards Suga became noticeably more distant. Of Tomo's warning he said to her not a word, though he might have been expected to pass it on to her before anyone else.

If the relationship with Suga had been a little further advanced Konno too might have had other ideas, but despite what seemed to others an almost suspicious degree of intimacy, once they were alone together Suga would keep him severely at a distance and refuse completely to relax with him. Konno, who during his life in lodgings had had relations with women older than himself, could not understand Suga's lack of forwardness, which seemed to suggest that any ill-considered advances would be coldly thrust aside. He failed to perceive the child-wife that lurked inside the older woman, and the more she fussed over him outwardly the more he was puzzled.

Autumn came, and almost immediately Suga took to bed with the hemorrhoids that always troubled her, but Konno made no move to approach her room.

Even in his youth Yukitomo, in whom the attitudes of male superiority that derived from his Kyushu samurai stock were deeply engrained, had never shown others the type of affection in times of illness that would have taken him with tender solicitude to Suga's bedside. Even where she lay in her room Suga could sometimes hear him scolding Tomo and the maids, out of temper at the inconvenience of having no one to attend to his needs.

At no other time did Suga need to battle so fiercely with her loneliness and her longing for her dead mother. Every time she went to the toilet she lost an alarming amount of blood, and she became too anemic even to stand.

"You're terribly pale . . . Is it really all right not to see the doctor?" Many times each day Tomo would come to Suga's bedside and ask such things, peering down at the paper-white face pressed against the pillow.

"I'm all right, thank you. It's always the same—another week and I shall be all right again," said Suga, looking up at Tomo feebly with eyes that had forgotten their usual gloom. To Suga, too, in her present weakened state, Tomo's face as she leaned towards her seemed to have lost its customary watchfulness and to be filled with motherly affection.

"Do you want to go to the toilet? You can't get there by yourself. Hold on to me . . ." Finding Suga with a grim expression and brows knitted with pain, trying to raise herself to her feet, Tomo hastened to support her by the arm.

"Thank you, Ma'am . . . But don't bother, I'll get someone to help me . . ."

"It's all right! Don't fret yourself."

Tomo put her arms around Suga's shoulders as she stood swaying on her feet. Clinging together, the two women staggered along the corridor, but after she had got Suga into the toilet Tomo suddenly noticed the bright red blood that had dripped onto the corridor floor and the hem of her own kimono. Her face twisted in a grimace as she gazed. The blood had come from Suga's body. She felt ashamed and soiled. Then, as though to blot out that feeling, she was overtaken by an indescribable sense of pity.

She took a piece of paper from inside the front of her kimono to wipe up the blood. The drops stained the corridor floor, countless drops like small red flowers. Tomo crouched down and wiped them away one by one. She could hear Suga groaning faintly inside the toilet.

"Are you all right? May I come in?"

The groans went on with no reply, so resolutely she opened the door and went inside.

3

The Stepsisters

Takao Shirakawa was lolling in a rattan reclining chair that he had taken out onto the second-story veranda of the annex of the house at Gotenyama. The room, a corner room facing southeast, was filled with sea air borne on the breezes that blew off the shore at Shinagawa and was the coolest in the whole large house. His grandmother had allotted it to him for his use when he came home from high school dormitory during summer vacation. He faced his university entrance examinations the following year, and she was concerned that he should have as comfortable a place as possible for his studies.

Whenever Takao took over the purely Japanese-style room with its fine timbers and its elegant bamboo blinds hanging from the eaves, it would suddenly acquire a bleak, uncared-for air, with books in Japanese and English lying in untidy piles on the floor where they had overflowed from the bookshelves, and inkstains on the surface of the mahogany desk, yet even this was a source of no small joy to Tomo, who saw in it a sign of her eldest grandson's love of learning. Having herself had barely enough education to enable her to read Chinese characters with the difficult pronunciations printed alongside, she bought Takao whatever books

155

he wanted, unstintingly, from her own purse, without even bothering to consult his grandfather Yukitomo. When the books were carried to his room and she watched his face as he contentedly turned the new pages, she felt the same satisfaction as a mother watching her young daughters gazing happily at fine new clothes.

A woman who hated to admit defeat, she could never reconcile herself to the mortifying fact that Takao's father Michimasa was a useless figure, apparently resembling neither her husband nor herself and living out his life in a kind of premature retirement. Yet his son Takao had shown a keen intelligence since early childhood and had taken in his stride the difficult hurdles of the entrance examinations that had finally got him to the best high school in the land, thereby restoring hope to Tomo and his grandfather, who had all but despaired of their descendants in direct line. For Yukitomo and Tomo it was a source of still greater joy that after the death of Michimasa's first wife in childbirth Takao had left his father's home and come to be raised under the wing of his grandfather and grandmother.

Brought up knowing no mother, in the home of a grandfather who wielded the absolute authority of a feudal lord, rocked in the arms of grandmother, grandfather's mistress, nurse, and other women in turn, Takao today cast about him a gloomy air of unsociability that was emphasized by his face with its hollow cheeks and its thick-lensed spectacles, a face entirely lacking in the freshness natural to youth.

"The young master's a lot fonder of books than he is of people, isn't he?" the young maids who came from the livelier low-class areas of Tokyo would say. "I wonder what he sees in it, doing nothing but read books all day long, Japanese books, foreign books—like an old man, I call it . . ."

Indifferent to the scorn of these girls—unable indeed to tell even their faces apart—Takao at his grandfather's home went on reading his books, sunk in a somber silence. But he was no bookworm infatuated with study for its own sake. Having a clear brain, he had only to take notes on his lectures and commit them roughly to memory to be able to face his examinations without any last-minute panic. Despite the studious label that he bore, most of the time he was in fact reading novels and plays, philosophical works and religious works, anything and everything as the fancy took him.

Even now the book that rested face down on his chest as he lay in the rattan chair was an English translation of a Greek tragedy, a small book with gold lettering embossed on its spine. He had just finished reading Sophocles' *Oedipus Rex*, and was turning the story over in his mind. The boy of whom it was predicted while he was still in his mother's womb that, as a man, he would kill his father and commit incest with his mother—the boy whose life was to have ended immediately at birth—miraculously survived, became king of an enemy state, attacked and defeated his father's kingdom, slew his father, and took his mother as consort, only to discover too late the obscene fate that had been lying in wait for him. Revolted by the shameful sin so unwittingly committed, he put out his own eyes and, blind, wandered forth on a journey of expiation . . . In its exposition of the inevitability of fate and the unconscious karma that the individual piles up for himself, the tragedy was in the same vein as the Buddhist tale of Prince Ajase or the medieval legends of Christianity.

If a son nowadays should actually sleep with his mother, Takao reflected, the act would undoubtedly seem shameful even after one had stripped away the exaggerations of religion and accepted morality. Nonetheless, he felt a strange, desolate kind of loneliness at never even having known a mother of his own flesh and blood who might have been the object of such illicit desires.

Miya, the young and beautiful woman whom he had been taught to call Mother as soon as he could talk had soon moved to another house, and nothing in his upbringing had given him any love or respect whatsoever for his father Michimasa; so that although there existed persons whom he might call Father and Mother, in practice they were no more to him than a remotely related uncle and his wife. The coldness of his grandparents' attitude to his father and the naked resentment that Michimasa showed for the love Yukitomo and Tomo lavished on him had combined with Michimasa's own complete lack of any fatherly warmth to harden Takao's heart abnormally in his boyhood.

Now his stepmother Miya lay at death's door in the hospital with her eighth child in her womb, stricken by a worsening of her laryngeal tuberculosis. His grandfather and grandmother had told him the news yesterday when he arrived home from the hostel, but it had not, honestly speaking, been enough to upset him.

Miya of the fair-skinned, meltingly soft body, of the cheerful, slightly nasal manner of speaking, of the gay laughter and the merry jokes, had never made him feel the cheerless ill will usually associated with the word "stepmother," yet neither did it seem likely that her sudden departure from the face of the earth would bring about any change in his own life. If Miya's death inspired any slight stirring of response in his heart, it was not caused by her decease as such but by the thought of how his stepsister Ruriko would grieve.

"Could I be in love with Ruriko, or is it purely brotherly love?" From King Oedipus's incest with his mother, his mind strayed to thoughts of Ruriko, and he had a sudden sense of impasse as though a barrier had reared up directly before his face.

How could someone who had never lived with his father and stepmother or known the force of love himself feel the true love of an elder brother for the younger sister and brothers borne by that mother and raised in a different house? In fact, he behaved toward Kazuya, the next youngest brother now studying at Keiō, and towards Tomoya and Yoshihiko who came after him, with almost the same distant politeness as to his cousins at his aunt Etsuko's; only to Ruriko, now in the fifth year at Tora-nomon Women's College did he for some reason feel a natural impulse—though the impulse itself was perhaps suspicious —to draw closer. He knew that the girl's striking beauty was an attraction for him. What he could not decide, however, was whether his beautiful stepsister attracted him in the same way as a beautiful flower or beautiful music or whether, as a female human being, she had sown in his lonely soul the seeds of first love.

Seized with an indefinable irritation, Takao shifted the book from his chest to the arm of the rattan chair with a gesture of unconscious force. As though fixing something unseen with his eyes he gazed up into the blue sky where the blazing rays of the sun had begun to yield to evening, then glanced casually at the lawn on the higher ground where the main building stood, and saw something that made him rise with a slight exclamation from his chair.

"Ruriko, here?" It was totally unexpected; Ruriko, whom he had assumed was at the hospital, was there, standing on the lawn in the garden.

She seemed completely unaware of his presence. Her hair, falling thick and free at the sides, was done up in a full "margaret" at the front and tied on top with a silk gauze ribbon in an irides-cent light blue like a cicada's wings. Her thin summer kimono of muslin with its pattern of lilies on white was tied with a red

159

sash, but her figure as she stood alone by a large clump of flowering pampas had a somehow dejected air as though she might be crying. Two large black swallowtail butterflies were tumbling over and over each other about the red ears of the pampas as though to symbolize Ruriko's feelings of anxiety.

This girl, he thought, was soon to lose her mother. At the idea of the cruel sorrow that would rack that frail body, an overwhelming pity welled up in Takao's breast.

"Ruriko."

Almost before he realized it he had put his hands on the wooden rail of the veranda and called to her in a loud voice, a voice with an unusual resonance.

Ruriko seemed not to realize where the voice calling her came from, and raising eyes still moist with tears looked about her till he called out again and she finally noticed him watching her from the second floor of the building halfway up the slope.

"Takao! Hello!" she called in a youthful voice. In the same moment she smiled gaily with the tears still in her eyes, and the grief shrouding her young body vanished like a thin garment slipping to the ground.

"They say Mother's in a bad way, don't they? When did you come from the hospital?"

"Just a while ago. Mother said to ask Grandfather to come. I was going to phone, but she said she wanted *me* to come. So I brought the message."

"I see . . . And did Grandfather say he'd go at once?"

"He's going after he's had his dinner and Dr. Akiyama's given him his neuritis injection. He says I'm to stay here tonight."

"I'll go with him. I was going to see her while it was still light, but a friend who's going back to the country tomorrow had lent me his notes, so . . ."

As he told the glib lie he looked down at Ruriko's face with its fair, almost translucent skin that showed no sign of the heat and the abundant black hair falling on either side of her slender neck.

"I'll join you in a moment."

"No, I'll come up. It'll be cooler there, won't it?"

Flashing a smile at him she turned her body swiftly as a swallow and disappeared behind the rock garden. Takao lowered himself into the reclining chair, a vaguely rueful smile still lingering on his gaunt cheeks. Almost immediately he heard the sound of light footsteps on the staircase and Ruriko appeared at the corner of the L-shaped veranda.

"Ah, it's nice and cool. I said it would be pleasanter here. What a nice breeze." She walked toward him as she spoke and seated herself unceremoniously on the floor beside the rattan chair. Just as her mother Miya had an air of worldly sophistication that somehow called to mind a geisha, so everything about Ruriko—her beautifully shaped eyes with the striking eyebrows, the rounded cheeks curving down toward the gentle firmness of the jaw, the slightly square shoulders on the short trunk with the firm, well-shaped buttocks—combined to give her a clearcut, pert air that suggested not so much the daughter of a good family as a young geisha, onetime dancing girl, who had tied her hair up in a knot in imitation of the style of a well-bred young lady. Compared with the other young girls among his relatives or the sisters of his friends, this neat femininity had for Takao the attractive fragility of some delicate bloom.

"Takao, when did you see Mother last?"

"Let's see—it was when I was home for the April vacation, so it must be about four months ago. She was well then, though."

"She was. It was just after that she had morning sickness. Mother always has it badly, doesn't she? So nobody realized what was really wrong with her."

At this point she seemed suddenly to be overtaken by sadness again and her voice became thick with tears.

"You'll see today. You'll get a shock. She used to be plump, but now she's so thin, and deathly pale; it suits her of course, but it's horrid all the same. And she can hardly talk. You can't put your face close to listen, either, as Grandmother and the others say it's catching if you go too near."

"Well, what do you expect with a disease?" said Takao frowning with obvious distaste. "Has she got as thin as all that?"

"Yes. She's literally only half the size she was."

In her twenties Miya had been slightly built, almost frail, with such a delicacy even of bone structure that Yukitomo would liken her, to her delight, to a young doe. But she was fond of alcohol, and every evening would drink with Michimasa, mixing indiscriminately large quantities of beer and saké; from around the time when she had her fourth child, Yoshihiko, she began to get fatter, until in the end one might have wondered just where the bones were concealed in such a well-covered body. As her already fair skin acquired a damask-like sheen, becoming ever sleeker and more satin-smooth with a look as though the fine-grained flesh might break like bean-curd at the touch, Michimasa would anger her by likening her to a white pig or a goose or other such unpleasant creatures. It was left to Yukitomo to give her in full measure the sensual gratification that she craved, to tell her that in China a woman of such soft and ample proportions was considered the height of feminine attractiveness, and that to hold her in his arms was to forget his age and ascend to the paradise of eternal youth.

Neither Takao nor Ruriko of course had any idea of the peculiar relationship between their grandfather and mother. Yet the grandfather who took her to the theater and department stores and bought her whatever she wanted was for Ruriko in her innocence far more to be loved and revered than the father who was always so irascible and self-willed. Next to her grandfather, she fancied that it was her eldest brother Takao whom she revered the most. Although both her father and her mother spoke contemptuously of Takao as "the eccentric," his sullenly taciturn, moody-looking face inspired in Ruriko a kind of trusting affection that made her prefer him by far to the more affable Kazuya, her elder brother by the same mother. The only thing that made her diffident with Takao was his difficulty in expressing himself and the infrequency of his smiles, which convinced her that this brother did not like her.

"They say Mother will never get well . . . The doctor and everybody else say so, but I don't believe it. Takao—you don't know what your real mother looked like, do you?"

"No, of course not. You know she died giving birth to me."

"Then I think you're lucky. It's better than having your mother die when you're grown-up like me."

"You just can't say either 'lucky' or 'unlucky.' "

"Yes, but . . ." She looked up at Takao as though to protest, when a black shadow brushed past their faces.

"Oh! It's those butterflies again!" she cried shrilly, beating at the air with the fan with a lacquered handle that she had in her hand.

There were two butterflies as before, black swallowtails, flitting about together as though they were mates, near the pillar at the corner of the room.

"Surely they're the ones that were fluttering about near you over by the pampas grass, aren't they?"

"Yes, they are. They've been following me around ever since I went out into the garden. Takao—those butterflies are horrid, they're like evil spirits. Evil spirits dressed in black, bringing me ill fortune."

Takao laughed in his desiccated voice.

"Look, look—they're back again! Takao—catch them, can't you?"

"How can I? They move faster than I do!" He took the painted fan from Ruriko's hand as he spoke and made a great sweep at one of the butterflies as it fluttered past, whereupon it skimmed along the floor and flew up again close to Ruriko's cheek.

"Ah! Do something! Takao!"

With a shrill cry like a small girl she pressed her face against Takao's chest. The hair spilled in waves down her back and her shoulders trembled like a small bird. An indescribably pleasant fragrance rose from her body as she pressed against him, and gently, almost unconsciously, his bony hand stroked the frail shoulders that looked as if they could be crushed at will in his grasp.

It was the light blue ribbon waving on Ruriko's hair as she clung to Takao's chest that caught Tomo's eyes in the rickshaw coming up the sloping drive from the gate.

Tomo, who had been to the hospital where Miya lay seriously ill, was on her way home after being told that there would probably be no turn for the worse that day or the next. Miya's request that Yukitomo should come to see her might mean that she had some last private message for him. If so, Tomo thought, it would be inappropriate for her to linger there, so she decided to leave things to Miya's relatives and go home.

Swaying in the rickshaw beneath the hot sun on the way back from the hospital at Onarimon, she was half-dozing despite herself when the vaguely sensual, coquettish cry of a young woman awoke her with a start. After long years married to Yukitomo she knew quite well when it was that a woman gave a cry like that. Glancing about her she found that they were already on the slope inside the gate, passing between thick rows of vegetation over which the pines spread their branches like parasols. She gave a rueful smile: for some years now even Yukitomo had been past the age when he could evoke that kind of cry from a woman. Had she been dreaming, then? She felt a spasm of distaste to find herself still so deeply enmired in the swamps of physical desire that scenes of sexual passion came to trouble her even in her dreams. She squeezed her eyes tightly shut, opened them wide again, and looked up towards the second floor of the annex where Takao would be. Would he be poring over a book with his usual surly, tired-looking face, or would he be taking a nap? In theory, there should be no mosquitoes in that room, but the idea that he might be bitten while he slept worried Tomo almost as though he were a small child still.

The first thing that met her gaze was Takao's gaunt face above the dark blue and white of his cotton kimono. Directly beneath his drooping head she could see a light blue ribbon sticking up in the air. No doubt about it, it was the ribbon that only a while ago she had seen fluttering about the hospital room and along the corridor on Ruriko's head. Her abundant hair, hanging loose, completely covered Takao's chest. One after the other Takao's long, bony fingers were tapping her shoulder as though he were playing a piano.

In the instant she saw them Tomo all but rose to her feet in the rickshaw. The sweat that beaded her skin in the heat seemed suddenly to chill, and her whole body began to tremble.

"Surely not! Surely . . .!" she muttered to herself almost as though in a delirium. And yet, was it really so impossible? Was she not Miya's daughter, after all? The child of that shameless woman . . .?

From the time when she first heard the unexpected news that

Miya's sickness was mortal Tomo had striven to rid herself of the persistent feelings of hatred and contempt that she had so far cherished for the other woman. Although the half-witted Michimasa might be no fit partner for her, there was still no excuse for the way, once her father-in-law started making advances, she let herself go and lived quite shamelessly, almost complacently, as a kind of favorite mistress. Had she been a woman in some profession whose duty was to entertain men it would have been different, but Miya had married into the family as an inexperienced girl, and to live in such violation of the claims of chastity branded her in Tomo's eyes as a female of the species with no more shame than a cat or a dog. Where shamelessness was concerned Yukitomo was the same, of course, but according to Tomo's old-fashioned code a man's morals were judged solely by his public behavior while a woman was expected to be faithful, and judged by this unfair standard Miya's conduct was more disgusting than Yukitomo's. Of the seven children that Miya had already borne Michimasa—Kazuya, followed by Ruriko, Tomoya, Yoshihiko, Namiko, Toyoko, and Katsumi—the fourth, Yoshihiko, was actually rumored to be Yukitomo's child, and the obvious affection that Yukitomo lavished on him afforded Tomo a bitter amusement. For dozens of years now she had known quite well that Yukitomo could have no more children; thanks to this fact, the family had never been troubled by problems of inheritance. Could he really believe, then, that quite suddenly when he was already past sixty he should have had a child by Miya? If so, men were hopelessly stupid where women were concerned. By now, moreover, he was far more attracted by Miya than by Suga, and the idea that he had actually had a child by her might have made the secret relationship with Miya into something still deeper and more comforting for him.

It was for this private reason that Yoshihiko, who was still at primary school, had been brought to live with his grandparents on the pretext that it was lonely while Takao was away at his school. Tomo had wondered with a sense of yet another spiritual burden whether Yoshihiko might not sooner or later become the center of a dispute over the inheritance, which made her feel that all things considered it might prove a good thing for Takao's future that Miya's life should end earlier than could have been foreseen.

Though his determination to have his own way might almost have summoned back the setting sun, even Yukitomo could not check Miya in her progress from life into death. Going from doctor to doctor, from hospital to hospital, he had exhausted every resource to no avail; there were times when Miya's unhappy fate seemed to Tomo almost like an inexorable dispensation of Providence.

Although that same Miya, secure under the shelter of Yukitomo's affection, had often shown scorn for Tomo, the kind of cruelty that could watch with a sneer of triumph while another human being died was quite foreign to Tomo's nature. The nearer Miya's life drew to its close, the more pity Tomo felt for her ignorance, and more than once she had held her in her arms as though she were her own daughter. Perhaps for the same reason Miya, who of late had grown pale, thin, and as insubstantial as a small girl, would often grasp her hand and say:

"I really feel awful towards you Mother, all the trouble I cause you . . ."

Tomo sensed in the words a hidden apology for all kinds of things that could never be expressed in speech, and each time would bow her head deeply in reply.

Could it be possible, even so, that Miya's daughter Ruriko was, in her turn, playing the role of seductress to Takao? Tomo dismissed the idea as absurd, but the girlish cry that she had

167

heard in the rickshaw, and the thick waves of Ruriko's hair against Takao's chest, spelled out for Tomo something incomparably dangerous that derived in equal measure from Yukitomo's lack of shame in crossing the barriers to the forbidden and from the licentiousness that lurked in Miya.

"Ruriko, were you in Takao's room a while ago?" she asked casually as they sat at dinner with Yukitomo, Takao, Ruriko, Yoshihiko and Suga.

"Yes, I was scared," she said looking at Takao over the bowl she held in her hand.

"What were you scared of?" asked Yukitomo from the head of the table.

"Black butterflies—they wouldn't leave me alone. Two of them, too."

"Really? Black butterflies . . ." said Suga, who had a taste for the macabre, opening wide her large eyes and knitting her brows. "What do you mean, 'wouldn't leave you alone'?"

"Well, at first they were fluttering about by the pampas grass at the foot of the rockery. I kept trying to shoo them away, but they wouldn't go. Then I saw Takao upstairs in the annex, so I ran up there. But then the two of them came after me . . ."

"Upstairs in the annex? Such a long way away, too!"

"You should have heard the scream she let out. It was enough to make me jump," said Takao.

"But I was scared! When Takao tried to drive them away with his fan they came flying up in my face."

"Perhaps the butterflies were under your spell because you're so pretty," said Suga quite seriously as she put more rice into the bowl that Yukitomo held out to her.

"No . . . I had the feeling rather that they'd come to let us know that mother was dying . . . though, actually, I phoned immediately and they said her condition hadn't changed."

Ruriko's eyes took on the significant look of a young girl who loves a mystery. Watching the steadiness and absolute absorption of her gaze, Tomo felt the fear that had assailed her in the rickshaw dispersing little by little.

Innumerable large moths were dancing in a blur of yellow wings about the electric lights suspended from the white ceiling of the hospital corridor. Some, tired of dancing, had come to rest with wings still open on the glass sliding doors. The breeze had dropped, and in the sultry heat of a midsummer night even the pungent smell of disinfectant in the hospital wing seemed dulled and heavy.

Wearing a pair of tinted glasses, with a silk gauze summer jacket over his kimono, Yukitomo walked briskly along the corridor, taking care to hold straight his now slightly bent back. A dull ache of neuritis still lingered in his left thigh, but more than this, for a man as self-willed as he, it was the intricate pain of having Miya taken from him that made his legs strangely loath to carry him to the bed where she lay on the threshold of death. So long as there had been any hope at all he had forced himself to believe that with all the resources of medicine he could restore her wanton flesh to health, but now that all hope had been frustrated the secret that he and Miya had guarded between them for so long had turned to a hollow, mocking laughter that echoed unceasingly in his ears. He had never experienced a sense of humble reverence for any woman other than the mother who had given him birth, yet still the Confucian creed that had been hammered into him in his youth forbade him to believe that it could be decent to have physical relations with the wife of his own flesh and blood. And yet, he told himself, Michimasa was a helpless parasite unable to get through life to his own feet; the fact that he had plenty of food and clothing and an attractive

169

woman as a wife was all part of the undeserved good fortune of having been born son to Yukitomo. His son was too stupid to realize the value of his wife nor did he love her; he merely slept with her and got her with children. If he himself had not given Miya love, it was unlikely that she would have stayed in this house as Michimasa's wife for close to twenty years. Even had she divorced Michimasa, what guarantee was there that her fate as a woman who had already failed once in marriage would have been happier than in fact it had? What Miya's husband had lacked in passion or in love Yukitomo had more than made up for.

The thought of having at the end to listen to words of repentance from Miya's lips was repugnant to Yukitomo. He wanted her to die as a woman of disrepute, dispensing still in the darkness of the night her licentious blend of odors and sensations. For seven days he had consciously avoided being left alone with her at the hospital, fearing vaguely the look she would turn on him as she died.

Outside Miya's room sat or squatted the relatives and family connections. The fans in their hands still moved lethargically from force of habit, but they were too overcome by heat and exhaustion to make any real conversation. The children had all gone home for the night.

"Where's Michimasa?" said Yukitomo, looking for him among Miya's mother, brother, and sisters as they rose to greet him.

"The master's not here today," said the foreman called Tomoshichi who had been staying at the hospital night and day. Yukitomo, secretly relieved, assumed a bad-tempered look and said nothing, at which Tomoshichi went on, as though to smooth things over, "He was tired from looking after the invalid . . . He must take a little rest, at least."

In fact Michimasa had not gone home but to see the first showing of that week's installment of an American film serial. Nearing fifty though he was, the cinema and the theater were still a pleasure that even his wife's death could not make him willingly forgo.

That morning the patient's condition had raised doubts that she would last the night, but the hospital director who had examined her some while ago had said that there would probably be no sudden change for a day or two; this Yukitomo learned, in fragments, from Miya's brothers and sisters and her mother, who in the midst of it all spotted Takao standing glumly behind Yukitomo in his gray uniform and exclaimed unctuously:

"Well, Takao! I didn't recognize you, you've grown so tall!"

To Takao, Miya's close relatives, gathered there with their worried expressions and forced tears as though they felt an obligation to grieve, had the artificiality of unskilled actors.

"Is she asleep?" asked Yukitomo.

"Oh no, she's awake. She hasn't seen Takao for such a long time . . . she's sure to be pleased." With which, Miya's mother took them into the sickroom.

It was a white-walled room with two windows. A high iron bed was covered with a thin layer of silk gauze quilts between which, so slender as hardly to suggest the presence of a human body, lay Miya.

Nurses in white uniforms with high collars were seated at the head and foot of the bed, gently stirring the air with round paper fans.

"Miya, here's Takao to see you," said Yukitomo seating himself by the bed and opening the front of his kimono to fan his chest. His voice was youthful and resilient.

Dully Miya raised her eyes which had been lightly closed and stared at Yukitomo. She seemed too tired to shift her gaze.

171

"Takao?" she said in a voice that had lost all its resonance. Takao peered out from behind his grandfather.

"How do you feel?" he said.

"My throat's so dry . . . I don't seem to have any voice . . ."

Her thin hand went up to feel at her throat. The eyes that had been little more than slits in her plump cheeks stood out dark and hollow against her face, which now that it was thin was youthful and attractive, and remarkably like Ruriko's.

"Is school over?"

"Yes, he came home from the dormitory yesterday," Yukitomo replied for him, busily flapping at his chest with the large black Chinese fan.

Standing where he was, Takao noticed his grandfather's fan motioning him towards the door so, glad of the opportunity to leave, he went out into the corridor. Yukitomo signaled to the two nurses with his eyes and they too, nodding, withdrew into the corridor.

Almost warily Miya looked in the direction that the white uniforms of the nurses had taken as they moved quietly towards the door.

"They've all gone outside," said Yukitomo. Drawing nearer to the bed, he fanned her with the fan he held in one hand while with the other he smoothed back the loose hairs that stirred over her forehead.

"You wanted to talk to me?"

"Not really to talk . . ."

She tried to put a smile into her wasted cheeks; for a moment the instincts of the beautiful female sought readmittance to their waxy whiteness, flickered there faintly, and instantly took off again for distant parts while Yukitomo watched them go like the frail, shining wings of a mayfly.

Miya frowned intently as though her throat was hurting her.

"But you've hardly been to see me at all!"

"We can't be alone together even if I come, can we?" said Yukitomo with deliberate brutality. "And besides, the doctor guarantees that you'll be leaving the hospital in two or three weeks' time. You'd better get out of this dismal hole as soon as you can ... We'll take you to the hot springs at Hakone or somewhere."

"I do hope so ... Somehow I feel discouraged. Papa, I wonder what you'll do if I die? I wonder if you'll be sad for me?"

"Don't talk nonsense, woman! I'm the one who's going to die first."

"I don't believe it," said Miya quite seriously in a hoarse voice.

So long beguiled by Miya's blend of cheerful playfulness and sulky pouting, Yukitomo found himself scared now by these classical features with the eyes that were so steady in their gaze. It occurred to him that it was unwillingness to see this face that had made him reluctant to come to visit her here.

"You know, Papa, I've worried about Yoshihiko. Somehow or other I feel easy about the others—Kazuya and Ruriko and Tomoya—but I get dreadfully anxious about Yoshihiko. Why this should be I'm sure I can't say ..."

"Yoshihiko's got less to worry about than the others. He's small but he's got a good head on him and he's sharp. If you're worried about him I could make an addition to the will for him, separately from the rest." Then he bent down close to where Miya's ear was buried in the pillow and whispered:

"Don't worry, Yoshihiko's *our* child, isn't he?"

Whether she had heard correctly or not, Miya suddenly shrank into herself and gave a small groan. A ripple of what could have been either physical pain or sorrow passed across her face. She herself did not know whether Yoshihiko was Michimasa's son or Yukitomo's. Her desperate attempt to make Yukitomo believe he

173

was his own child had been a ruse to attach his love more closely to herself than to Suga. Even now, she still did not realize that she was to die. But in her body now that it lay near death, drained of all material and sexual desires, the spirit had unconsciously and unaccountably begun to make itself felt. That she had passed off Yoshihiko on Yukitomo as his own child was a thorn nagging at her flesh. She would have liked to tell him; but now that they were alone together she knew that by its very nature the thing could not be confessed. The anguish that shrouded her face came from the pain of having to lock away the secret within herself for all eternity.

At the hospital around dusk on the fifth day following this meeting, Miya breathed her last. Her body was transferred to the main house at Gotenyama, where the whole establishment was given over to an ostentatious wake that lasted two nights and was followed by an imposing funeral at a temple in Azabu.

"It's not as though a wife or an heir had died. It's too impressive for a mere daughter-in-law. I'd wager that Mr. Shirakawa intended it as a rehearsal for his own funeral," said the close acquaintances and tradespeople who came to the house.

Michimasa showed little sign of missing the wife who had borne him seven children in rapid succession, and continued as ever to amuse himself at the theater, the cinema, and other such places.

"Miya had too much to say for herself; next time I want a well-behaved woman, the kind that will bow and scrape a little," he would say whenever the question of a successor arose.

Even with nurses and maids, it would be impossible for a widower to direct the upbringing of so many children unaided. Miya had been dead for barely half a year before Tomo was obliged to concern herself with finding a third wife for Michimasa.

On one occasion before Michimasa's first marriage, as she was consulting a fortune-teller concerning compatibility and such matters, she had been told that her son's horoscope foretold trouble with women, and had thought to herself wryly that Michimasa scarcely had enough spirit to suffer in that particular way, but it occurred to her now that to be preceded to the grave by two wives was undoubtedly "trouble with women" of a kind.

It was true that Miya's death had lightened Tomo's burden by bringing to a natural end the illicit relationship between father and daughter-in-law that had caused her such constant trepidation lest it come to light, but her determination was all the stronger that the third bride should be an utterly serious-minded woman with none of Miya's jezebel qualities.

However deficient Michimasa might be as a man there were plenty of go-betweens to suggest potential partners with an eye to the Shirakawa fortune. From amongst these Tomo chose a middle-aged spinster who taught household management at a school for girls. Tomoe by name, she was broad-shouldered and had a narrow forehead but her complexion, at least, was fair. Michimasa did not care for the name Tomoe and as soon as she was installed in the house changed it to the more elegant "Fujie." Fujie was strict with the children and served Michimasa with the deference due to a lord and master.

When she paid her first visit to the house at Gotenyama following the wedding ceremony, Yukitomo treated Fujie with great affability and tact, but it was clear at a glance not only to Tomo but to Suga as well that she was not the kind of woman to replace Miyo.

"The new wife seems to be a steady kind of person, doesn't she?" Suga remarked casually one day as she was sitting facing Tomo across the brazier. Despite herself an equivocal smile flickered on one side of her face.

"Yes—I suppose she does," Tomo replied with equal composure as she lit the tobacco in her long pipe. She knew only too well from past experience that if she let herself be tempted into speaking too freely her words would be flung back at her from Yukitomo's with a weight of significance she had never intended.

"But if she's a teacher of household management, she should be good at tightening up the household finances. They'll be finding it quite hard going from now on, I expect," Suga said, tapping out a similar long pipe against the edge of the brazier.

Tomo was left to infer from Suga's roundabout way of putting it that she referred to the considerable sums of money Yukitomo had privately been giving to Miya. Michimasa had never dreamed that all kinds of extravagances over and above the routine household expenditure were being paid for in exchange for his wife's body, but now that Fujie had replaced Miya it was unlikely that the money would flow so freely from Yukitomo's side.

Yukitomo decided that Ruriko in addition to Yoshihiko should be brought to live at the big house. It might be that in this young girl who every day grew more attractive and more graceful he was seeking to recapture the Miya that had once been, yet toward her grandfather Ruriko employed none of her mother's wheedling familiarity nor did she show the slightest consciousness of the beauty that struck others so forcibly.

"Miss Ruriko is still just an immature girl," Suga would sometimes say admiringly to Tomo, with the hidden implication that Ruriko's nature was not like her mother's.

However many favors Yukitomo might bestow on Ruriko, Tomo had no fears on that score at least, though when she thought of Takao it was undoubtedly a relief to know that Ruriko by nature was so wanting in her mother's conscious desire to charm.

Takao, who that summer had in the natural course of events

gained admission to the history department of Tokyo Imperial University, had come back to the house at Gotenyama; he had been given the room upstairs in the annex as his study and traveled every day to the university campus in the Hongo district. Ruriko had left women's college and was going about taking lessons in the tea-ceremony, flower arrangement, and the piano, so that sometimes she would find herself accompanying Takao on his way to or from the university. One evening as he alighted from the rear exit of a streetcar he saw her, wearing a kimono of printed silk with an arrow-feather pattern and carrying in one hand some flowers wrapped in a piece of oiled paper, leaving the front exit of the same car. He did not hail her, however, but walked along behind her at a distance of some two yards.

"Miss Shirakawa—I bet you don't know you've got the young master walking after you!" The voice that hailed Ruriko on the slope that led up to the big house belonged to Tomoshichi the foreman, who was wearing a workman's jacket with the name "Shirakawa" in white on the dark blue of its collar.

"What? Really?"

She turned and recognized Takao who was screwing up his eyes as though dazzled by the light.

"The young master's a wicked one all right," cackled Tomoshichi. "It's lucky it's your sister, or she'd be annoyed. Walking like that just behind an attractive young lady without saying anything . . ."

Tomoshichi, it seemed, had just been given a drink at the Shirakawas', and his eyes in his neat featured face were faintly red around the rims. How pleasant it would be, he thought, if only Takao could take a joke, but Takao, surly-faced, made no response at all so Tomoshichi hurried on past with a disgruntled air.

"What an unpleasant foreman that is," Ruriko muttered with

177

an air of distaste. "Grandfather seems to think a lot of him, but I hate him. You know, he's always teasing the maids in the kitchen." Even in the way they behaved to the employees and tradespeople there was a great difference between Ruriko and Miya, who had had the easygoing affability characteristic of her plebeian background.

Takao made no reply but walked rapidly on up the slope, this time by her side.

The Waiting Years

At the top of Kagura Hill two child geishas in kimonos of printed silk with long sleeves were playing New Year's shuttlecock. The older geisha who stood looking on wore a multi-colored evening kimono, although it was still light, and was lifting the hem slightly as though deliberately to show off the fine-spotted undergarment beneath. Both kimono and sash were of unusually good quality for a geisha of this quarter, while the large battledore that hung from her hand, with its picture of the Kabuki actor Kichiemon in a well-known role, must have cost at least twenty yen at the Yagen-bori fair.

Thanks to the war in Europe that was already in its third or fourth year, shares in military supplies and ships had shown an astonishing rise. The geisha houses were flourishing as a result of the wartime boom, and it was even rumored that a certain shipbuilder who had made his fortune overnight had given a former Osaka geisha a kimono with the pattern at the hem studded with great diamonds. If even the geishas in a second- or third-rate quarter like this could get themselves up in this fashion, what must it be like in the first class districts? As she walked past, Tomo gazed at the geisha's profile with its smartly swept up sidelocks and found herself calling to mind first one then another face from the past, faces of geishas of the Shimbashi quarter with which she had had no contact for some twenty years by now. At the time when Yukitomo had been a high-ranking official in the Metropolitan Police Department, geishas from Shimbashi had always been summoned to entertain guests at the parties he held at his official residence. Some of them were old acquaintances of Yukitomo's and often one would come to pay her respects in the daytime, clothed in a respectable striped kimono and carrying some dainty, toylike present, accompanied by the proprietress and chief maid of the teahouse. It occurred to Tomo now that most of them, so mature in their sober kimonos in colors that firmly rejected any telltale suggestion of red, could have been little more than twenty years of age.

And Suga and Yumi, who at that time still did their hair in girlish hairstyles, were now long past forty while Takao and Kazuya, who were then not even born, were old enough to be going to the university. Even Naoichi, Yumi's child by Iwamoto, was attending Hitotsubashi Commercial College by now. When Iwamoto had without warning died of typhus while the children were still small, Yumi had belatedly taken up flower arrangement, become a teacher, and with the help of Yukitomo and Tomo had managed to give Naoichi an education. Tomo's destination today was the small house in a backstreet off Kagura Hill where Yumi lived. She had not come to see Yumi herself, who would be out teaching now that the New Year's holiday was over, but a young woman called Kayo who occupied a small room on the second floor of her home.

She slid open the ill-fitting lattice door of the poorly-built, semi-detached house and called out, whereupon an elderly woman with pure white hair and a clear-eyed gaze emerged from the dim interior busily wiping her hands as though she had been doing the washing. Peering out through the door she recognized Tomo and immediately knelt and bowed low to the floor.

"Well, I never—Mrs. Shirakawa from the big house! Oh dear, and the children have all had colds since the end of the year, so I'm sure Yumi hasn't even been to pay her respects yet. But a happy New Year to you . . ." And giving Tomo no time to return her greetings she deferentially ushered her into the house. It was Yumi's elder sister Shin, now a widow too, whose presence in the house was what enabled Yumi to leave behind |her youngest daughter, who was still at primary school, and go out to teach.

"I'm afraid we've put you to a lot of trouble," said Tomo. "But I was glad at least to hear it was an easy delivery."

"Yes—do you know, we were so worried, you'd have thought even Yumi had never had any children herself. But then, it was an easy birth after all! And a lovely, plump, goodlooking boy it is, too. I can't say myself, but Yumi says there's no doubt about it, he's the very image of Mr. Kazuya."

"I'm ashamed of him, behaving like this when he's only a student still . . . But then, Kazuya hasn't got a real mother. It seems that leaves its mark in all kinds of ways . . ."

"Oh, but it's the kind of thing that often happens with the gentlemen, isn't it? Why, Kayo said if only she had two pairs of hands, she could earn her living and keep the child somehow."

"Yes, of course . . . but then, you see, the agent at the estate at Kiyojimachō has been good enough to arrange things. It's more or less agreed that he shall be taken by a very respectable office worker and his wife who've been wanting a child. They haven't said anything about it's being Kazuya's child, but— well, it seems they know where he comes from and they appear to be pleased about it. They should be coming to fetch him in another month or so."

"What a lucky boy, really, to have his grandmother look after everything for him. But after all, though he's not the eldest he's your grandson, and you'll be expecting a lot of him in the years to come, won't you?"

Making tea as she spoke, Shin kept a watchful eye on Tomo. Neither Yumi nor Naoichi seemed to attach much importance to the fact, but it was Tomo and not Yukitomo who, come rain come shine, had looked after Yumi and her children since she had been left a widow. Even though the late Iwamoto was her nephew, to put herself out so on behalf of a former mistress of Yukitomo's was not something to be dismissed lightly. Shin knew that the prosperity of the Shirakawas was really founded less on any ability of Yukitomo's than on the thankless labors of Tomo, and she would reflect ruefully on the indifference of her own relatives. Kayo, the maid from Michimasa's who was now lodging upstairs and who was a mere girl of eighteen, had got herself pregnant by Kazuya, now a student in the economics department of Keio University, and it was Tomo who had arranged that she should have the child here.

With Shin leading the way Tomo pulled herself by the bannister up the steep and narrow flight of stairs that led up from a corner of the parlor.

"Here's Mrs. Shirakawa from the big house to see you," Shin declared with one hand ready to open the sliding door that blocked the way at the top of the stairs.

"Gracious!" exclaimed a youthful voice, and Kayo came into sight as she sat up in the bed where she had been lying with her baby beside her.

"It's all right—you just stay lying down now," said Tomo from behind Shin as she followed her into the room, but by then Kayo had already clutched together the front of her kimono over her ample, white-skinned bosom and was waiting as deferentially as when she had been in service at Tsunamachi.

"First, I must congratulate you on a safe delivery. I meant to come rather sooner, but the New Year, you know . . ."

"Oh yes, it's the very busiest time for everyone, of course," Kayo continued with a look of nostalgic concern for the households at Tsunamachi and Gotenyama. The flesh of her slight shoulders that had always been so plump and of her fair-skinned cheeks with the peach-like bloom seemed somehow less full today, which, with the weariness about her eyes, gave her girlish body a new womanly appeal and pathos.

"I have to thank you for letting me have the baby here in peace."

"Yes, she was really lucky," put in Shin. "Kayo's mother isn't her real mother either, it seems, so I suppose it would be difficult to tell her about this kind of thing. And the lady at Tsunamachi is no blood-relation of Kazuya's either, is she . . . ? Kayo says she owes everything to Mrs. Shirakawa at the big house . . ."

"The baby—is he asleep?" Without getting up Tomo edged across the *tatami* to where the baby had been set down on the edge of the checkered silk bedding.

"He's just had a good feed, you see . . ." said Kayo half apologetically and gently shifted the gauze in which the baby's chin was buried so as to let Tomo see the whole of his tiny face.

"Gently, gently, he musn't be woken up, now," Tomo said reprovingly to Kayo as she leaned cautiously across to peer at the baby. The baby, who was not yet twenty days old, and still had no eyebrows, was a flabby mass of innocence that looked as though it would sink without resistance if one pressed it with a finger. The indistinct, soon-to-disappear creases in its forehead and cheeks gave an almost animal texture to the flesh. Yet even from this tiny, amorphous lump of flesh there emerged unmistakably, in the area around the forehead and the bridge of the nose, the face of Kazuya. In the deep furrow of the eyelids there even lurked a definite hint of Takao's face as a small child. No doubt about it, the child carried on the Shirakawa line. At the thought, a shiver of revulsion ran down Tomo's back. If this had been Kayo's child by Takao rather than by Kazuya she would surely never have dreamed of taking it from the cradle and giving it away to strangers. Only too well she knew without having to weigh things up in her heart the discrepancy in her love for those two grandchildren—Takao whom she had reared with her own hand and Kazuya, fruit of Miya's womb.

"There's a likeness, isn't there?" said Shin, looking at Tomo and deliberately avoiding any mention of Kazuya's name. Tomo nodded without speaking then said:

"He's a dear baby and he has a beautiful complexion."

She felt in a way that it was cruel to speak to Kayo now of having the baby adopted, but she knew that she could not come here so often herself, and it seemed that if she kept everything brief and free of emotion Kayo too, who was young after all, would not show herself unduly attached to the baby.

"I have such a lot of milk—I shan't know what to do when the baby's gone . . ." To hear her talk in this vein with no apparent grief at all only made Tomo feel more pity for her than ever.

In the end Tomo left without seeing the baby awake. She felt her way cautiously down the same dark stairs and was going out to the gate when Kayo, who had come with her to see her off, said as she helped her on with her coat:

"I don't think you're quite yourself, are you ma'am?"

"Why . . .? Do I look as though there's something . . .?" asked Tomo.

"No, I just had the idea you'd got rather thinner. But perhaps it's my imagination." And she smiled girlishly.

"To tell the truth, I had a cold at the end of the year. I don't seem to have shaken it off completely, you see." She paused a moment. "Never mind—it'll soon get better. It's already January too, so this cold can't last long now," she added as she went out through the gate. Her hand on the lattice door, Shin looked up at the narrow strip of leaden sky showing between the eaves and said:

"The clouds are getting awfully low. I only hope it doesn't start to snow before you get home . . ."

Tomo disliked traveling long distances by rickshaw. Having grown up in an age without streetcars or trains, she had always been proud of her strong legs, but she hated too to think that she could no longer do what she had when she was younger. For one who took upon herself all the supervision of land and houses and spent one half of every month outside the house, strong legs were a sign of good health that also, by helping to keep her inner self constantly on its guard, had a surprisingly weighty significance in her relations with Yukitomo and Suga. In a large household comprising Yoshihiko, Suga, and three maids in addition to Yukitomo and Takao, Tomo found herself giving constant priority to the affairs of others. They might all have been convinced that Tomo was immortal, for all the thought that any of them gave to her own health.

Yukitomo would dismiss the question airily with "Grandmother's one of those women who never get sick," an attitude that was shared by the young grandchildren and even by Suga, who might have been expected to show a more womanly concern but in fact was solely preoccupied with her own delicate health, complaining as though half resentfully:

"I envy the mistress her strength."

The stout-hearted Tomo's constitution was not in fact weak, nor once throughout the years had she had an illness of any seriousness, but this was more than half due to a fierceness of spirit that made her ever anxious to press on, ignoring any feeling of indisposition. She did in fact suffer from dizziness and a tendency to neuritis. Regularly for the past five or six years, at the hottest period of summer, she had had water on the knee and a feeling of breathlessness, but regularly too, when the cool breezes began to blow, the swelling would subside and the overpowering lethargy would leave her, so that however often her married daughter Etsuko advised her to consult a reliable doctor she made no move to go. She dreaded being told that she had some chronic ailment, lest this should cause a crack in the armor of her spirit and start insidiously wearing her down in mind and body. The mere idea that illness might leave her an invalid, immobile in one room of that chilly great house, filled her with an intolerable sense of indignation. Sometimes as she watched Yukitomo sitting, every day from morning to night on his cushion with the back-rest, taking his own temperature, gargling, putting drops in his eyes and otherwise coddling himself with the same greed for life as the ancient Chinese monarchs who sent out men to seek the elixir of youth, she would remind herself that her husband was a full twelve years older than herself. Even if he lived to be eighty she herself would still not be seventy. She must hold on until then. Until then, she must not go under to Yukitomo. And along with the idea that her life must triumph over Yuki-tomo's, there came an icy sense of desolation at the coldness of a relationship that could foster such an idea, at its remoteness from all normal ideas of the bond between husband and wife.

The kindly, unthinking inquiry after her health that Kayo had just made at the gateway had come as a shock. Her winter cold had indeed lingered on, half forgotten, in the usual New Year's rush of visitors, but recently a heaviness in the legs that she normally never felt in winter had slowly crept up to around the pit of her stomach; even at the New Year's feasts she could not bring herself to have a second helping of the rice cake in soup that she liked so much.

"Well, ma'am!—is that all you're having?" the maid serving them had asked in surprise.

"My teeth don't seem to be up to it today," Tomo had said, passing the matter off lightly. The others went on plying their chopsticks untroubled, it seemed, by the exchange. Tomo was if anything relieved by this lack of attention, which was preferable to having somebody show concern about her lack of appetite, thus drawing Yukitomo's attention to her, yet the failure of the assembled family to turn on her a single glance made sensitive by love, though nothing new, gave her the same sense of isolation as the deaf feel in their silent world.

She had been saddened during the past few years to see Takao, whom she had held in her arms as a baby and on whom as he grew up she had lavished all her love, growing visibly more distant. It might be that the care with which Tomo had married off Ruriko to a bank employee in the Kansai area not long after she left women's college had, by depriving him of what promised to be his first love, inflicted on him a wound of which he could not speak. Although he knew that such a love for his half-sister could come to nothing, the unnecessary haste with which his grandmother had got Ruriko married had, indeed, taken him aback with the sharpness of her insight into his hidden feelings, and the shock of having been caught off his guard had gradually stripped his attitude to her of its easy confidence. A vague sense of revulsion towards Tomo's acuity took root in him. While he ceased trying to have his own way with her, he also grew visibly impatient with the playful digs at his weaknesses that were her way of showing love, and thrust her away from him.

Tomo realized that in exchange for her success in putting Ruriko, willy-nilly, beyond the reach of Takao's affections she had lost the old frankness with which he had always bared his feelings to her. It was sad, but it could not be helped. However much she loved Takao it was obvious that Ruriko was one thing he could not have. She had seen too much immorality and license in Yukitomo's life to tolerate the idea of its affecting her beloved grandson, however wary he might become of her.

187

Yet why, she asked herself, should she be obliged to spend all her life entangled with such distasteful affairs? Why should things that she wished no part in happen, or threaten to happen, among those she was closest to and loved the most. It was a problem that admitted of no solution under any theories that her mind could conceive. Some power, outside herself, had given life to her and determined the course that she should take. Finally, of late, Tomo had begun to suspect that it was indeed a matter of inexorable destiny, to sense as a reality the existence of something stronger and more binding still than the code of human conduct she had guarded so stubbornly.

"*Namu Amida Butsu, Namu Amida Butsu . . .*" Effortlessly the muttered invocation of the Buddha found its way to Tomo's lips; sometimes it went on and on unconsciously with an intensity that made them burn.

By the time she alighted from the streetcar at the stop nearest to home the confining membrane of gray sky had broken and a fine snow like cotton fluff had begun to sift down.

"So it *is* going to snow," Tomo muttered to herself as she crossed the streetcar tracks on legs so heavy that her clogs seemed to cling to the road at each step and her breath escaped from her body in heavy gasps.

I must be very tired, she thought. She normally disliked going by rickshaw but with her legs as they were today it was obviously impossible for her to climb the long, gentle slope that led home. She set off walking towards the point, at the corner where the slope joined the road with the streetcar tracks, at which rickshaws were usually to be found waiting for fares. But the snow must have found them customers already, for no rickshaws were to be seen, nor the rickshaw men with blankets round their shoulders, warming themselves by their fire.

However irritating it might be, there was no one to complain to. Resigning herself to the inevitable, Tomo slowly began to drag her reluctant legs up the gentle incline. There had been no rain for some days, and already the fine snow had begun to smudge the roadway with white and to powder the branches of the trees above the stone embankment bordering one side of the slope and the gray roof tiles of the small rows of shops that lined the other. The lamps that were just being lit shone orange on the snow and a smell of fish cooking for the evening meal mingled with the smoke that here and there drifted out from beneath the eaves.

The hand that held the umbrella was numbed by the snow, and the climb, lifting one foot laboriously after the other, was so wearying that many times she halted and took a deep breath. The small houses she saw before her each time she halted were an undistinguished collection of secondhand shops, grocers, general stores and the like, yet the orange light from their electric lamps had an infinite brightness, and the odors of cooking appealed to the senses with an ineffable richness and warmth that shook Tomo's heart to the core. Happiness—a small-scale, endearing, harmonious happiness—surely dwelt here beneath the low-powered lamps in the tiny rooms of these houses. A small-scale happiness and a modest harmony: let a man cry out, let him rage, let him howl with grief with all the power of which he was capable, what more than these could he ever hope to gain in this life?

Tomo felt a sudden, futile despair at herself as she stood there in the road alone in the snow, loath to go on, with her gray shawl drawn up close about her neck and an open umbrella held in the hand that was frozen like ice. Everything that she had suffered for, worked for, and won within the restricted sphere of a life whose key she had for decades past entrusted to her wayward husband Yukitomo lay within the confines of that unfeeling,

189

hard, and unassailable fortress summed up by the one word "family." No doubt, she had held her own in that small world. In a sense, all the strength of her life had gone into doing just that; but now in the light of the lamps of these small houses that so cheerlessly lined one side of the street she had suddenly seen the futility of that somehow artificial life on which she had lavished so much energy and wisdom.

Was it possible, then, that everything she had lived for was vain and profitless? No: she shook her head in firm rejection of the idea. Her world was a precarious place, a place where one groped one's way through the gloom; where everything one's hand touched was colorless, hard, and cold; where the darkness seemed to stretch endlessly ahead. Yet at the end of it all a brighter world surely lay waiting, like the light when one finally emerges from a tunnel. If it were not there waiting, then nothing made sense. She must not despair, she must walk on; unless she climbed and went on climbing she would never reach the top of the hill.

Taking a deep breath, she shifted the heavy umbrella in her hand. Tightly clasped in her other hand was the cloth hold-all containing her papers. She looked up, and saw the gently sloping road stretching up far away from her. She thought she had covered three-quarters of the way, but it was still scarcely a half.

She closed the umbrella to use as a walking stick and pulling the shawl up over her head trudged on once more.

The following Saturday Etsuko came with her youngest daughter Kuniko to stay the night, their first visit of the New Year. Tomo was up as usual, but had felt sick since early morning and could scarcely take any food. By the time she had finally reached home on the evening of the snowfall she had barely been able to take more than a single pace without resting. Opening the lattice door of the side entrance and seating herself on the

190

edge of the raised floor inside the hall, she felt faint and unable to speak.

When Suga came out to welcome her home, Tomo did not look up but gestured with her hand and said:

"Warm water."

Startled to see Tomo with the snow-covered shawl still over her head Suga, when she brought the water, had peered into Tomo's face as she sat hunched forward on the step.

"Is something wrong?" she asked.

"Don't worry, it's nothing. I'm just a little tired," said Tomo without opening her eyes. "Please don't tell the master."

She went to bed early that night but was up as usual the following day. She knew that Etsuko was coming on Saturday and felt she must not under any circumstances take to her bed before then. A dread lest she should not be able to get up again put strength into her weary limbs.

Etsuko's husband Shinohara was by now a leading barrister. His relations with his wife Etsuko were good and his attitude as son-in-law to Yukitomo and Tomo left nothing to be desired, so that even Yukitomo who scorned his own son Michimasa was obliged to pay him a grudging respect. Partly out of deference to the other's position as a man, he rarely objected to any suggestion made by Shinohara. When something occurred that was beyond her own powers to deal with, Tomo would let Shinohara know via Etsuko and have him make the suggestion to Yukitomo.

To Etsuko, who before her marriage had been a well-bred girl with little conscious charm, marriage had not brought the same cares as to Tomo, and even in middle age she still preserved the purity of outlook, free of unsuspected depths, of a girl brought up in sheltered surroundings. There were times when this seemed to Tomo a sign of a happiness granted in recompense for her own misfortunes, but there were other times when, grumbling to

Etsuko about domestic matters involving Yukitomo and Suga, she felt discouraged by the lack of complexity and sensitive appreciation of her own feelings in her daughter's response. Generally speaking, Tomo had never felt a desire to shift the burden from her own shoulders to Etsuko's, but today was an exception and she awaited Etsuko's arrival with eagerness.

As they came into the room where Yukitomo sat leaning against his back-rest—Etsuko in her black crepe kimono decorated with the family crest and tied with a splendid sash embroidered with a design of bamboo and sparrows on a reddish-brown ground, leading by the hand Kuniko in a gay long-sleeved kimono of printed silk crepe—Tomo's heart gave such a leap of gladness that it startled even herself.

"Well, here they are!" said Yukitomo. "A happy New Year to you! And how old would Kuniko be now? When you've got too many grandchildren you can't remember all their ages!" He chuckled. "I'm getting terribly old. This year may easily see me saying farewell to this world . . . Where's Shinohara? Not with you? And here I'd got the *go* board all ready . . . A New Year's meeting of the Lawyers' Association? I see. If he's president he can hardly miss it, can he?"

To watch Etsuko's face, so like his as she sat demurely before him holding her head high on her long swan-like neck, seemed to give Yukitomo pleasure and he talked a lot, almost as though trying consciously to please her. Wishing to humor their aging master, Suga and the maids too took turns in praising Etsuko's hairstyle and the pattern of Kuniko's kimono.

That afternoon, when Kuniko had gone out to play shuttlecock and battledore with the maids and her contemporary Namiko, who had been invited over from Tsunamachi, Tomo said to Etsuko:

"There was such a good view of Mt. Fuji from upstairs yesterday. Come and have a look," and she led her as casually as possible upstairs to the front of the second floor.

From the veranda Mt. Fuji was visible, pale blue in the west, but Etsuko gave it no more than a brief glance before saying:

"Mother, is there something you want to talk about?" She seated herself on the *tatami* near the veranda. She knew after so many years that it was her mother's habit to take her aside without seeming to make a point of it whenever she had something private to say.

"You know, I don't think I'm very well."

"I'm sure you're not. I've been worrying because you looked rather tired. What's the matter exactly? Have you been to the doctor?"

"No," said Tomo with a vigorous shake of her head. "Mr. Suzuki comes to examine Grandfather at least once every three days, but I've no faith in a doctor who's more like a male geisha. I was waiting till you came, to tell the truth. For once I thought I'd get a decent doctor to have a look at me."

" 'Waiting,' indeed! Mother, there's no excuse for waiting where illness is concerned. Why didn't you phone me sooner?"

"Now, now, don't take it to heart so," said Tomo with a little laugh as though reproving Etsuko for getting too serious.

It would have seemed exaggerated to telephone just for that, and to write a letter specially would have alarmed people. She had not minded waiting because she was sure that Etsuko would be coming today. And little by little she began to tell her of the new symptoms she had been having since the end of the year.

"Look how swollen my leg is." As she spoke she stretched a leg out in front of her, pulled up the skirt of her kimono, and pressed the shin with her finger. The yellowed skin of her leg sank beneath the touch to form a pallid indentation that remained even after she had removed the finger.

193

"You see?" she said, glancing intently at Etsuko with eyes that were slightly bloodshot.

"It's puffy," said Etsuko with a frown as she looked at the dull white hollow of her eyes. I'm sure it's the kidneys, she thought. She felt a sense of shock at Tomo's unaccustomed behavior in stretching out her leg in front of her; it was something that even she, her daughter, had never seen before. It was as though the mother she saw before her now had put aside everything about which she normally cared.

"We'd better fetch the doctor as soon as possible. Shall I speak to Father about it?"

"Yes—yes, I think it would be all right for you to do it . . ." She lowered her eyes warily. "But I don't want him to think I said something."

"Surely you don't need to worry about that kind of thing?"

"But I do. You're so logical, but this house doesn't work by logic."

"Yes, but it depends on what it's about, surely. I'm sure even Father wouldn't be so unreasonable. Or shall I get my husband to tell him?"

"If you could—yes, that would be best, I feel. But he's busy, isn't he? I wonder when he could find time?"

"I'll get him to come tomorrow if necessary. Then he can say you don't seem to be very well and fetch a friend of his who's a doctor at the university hospital."

"I'm sure I could go to see him without bringing him all the way here."

"No, Mother. You don't need to consider others so. I've always told you, haven't I—since you're forever saying your legs are so heavy, you must, absolutely, be examined by a good doctor and take it easy until you're better."

"Oh really, I'm sure it's nothing serious . . ." She made a

vague attempt at undoing the effect of what she had said, but suddenly her face changed as though she had looked down into a great abyss.

"You know, Etsuko, there's one more thing I'd like to ask of you. This is one thing that I really hope you'll agree to."

"What is it, Mother?" Etsuko had hunched her shoulders defensively at the gravity of her mother's expression.

"Look, I don't like to talk like this, but supposing when the doctor examines me he says my illness is incurable—"

"Mother—don't be silly."

"Wait—this is only a theory. Just *supposing*, I'm saying . . . Everybody has to die sometime or other, so it can't do any harm just to think about it. Well then—if it turned out that the illness was incurable, I don't suppose for a moment the doctor would tell me, and nobody else in the house would want to tell me either. But that idea bothers me. If it's the kind of illness I'm going to die of, I want to know definitely. You see, there are things I must do once I know I'm going to die. If you and the others were to feel sorry for me and say nice things to keep me happy and if I died before I could do what I have to, I should never forgive you. Etsuko you're my daughter, I'm sure you understand my nature better than anybody. I feel that at least with you and your husband I can talk about anything freely, so . . . you will, won't you? I rely on you!"

Her voice was quiet as though she were chatting about nothing in particular, but as Etsuko listened she felt an indefinable pressure gradually bearing down upon her. The acuity with which her mother seemed, almost, to foresee her own death scared her.

"Very well. But I'm sure it's all unnecessary," she said, forcing a bright smile. Tomo, too, wrinkled her heavy eyelids in a smile to match her daughter's deception.

"Well," she said. "If we've finished talking shall we go downstairs? If we're too long, that Suga will start drawing conclusions again."

She placed her hands on her knees and slowly raised herself to her feet. Then, as she started to walk she turned to look at Etsuko and murmured:

"He got the better of me after all, didn't he? Grandfather got the better of me . . ."

For a moment, Etsuko could not grasp exactly what she meant.

That evening, after Etsuko and her daughter had left, Tomo took to her bed complaining she felt cold, and the next morning was no longer able to get up. Etsuko's husband looked in to see her when he came to pay his New Year's visit.

"Father," he said to Yukitomo, "Mother's condition seems to have changed a bit. Why don't you have my friend Inezawa have a look at her? It won't be any use making a fuss once it's too late."

He spoke in a frank, easy manner as the two of them were relaxing over the *go* board. Yukitomo nodded.

"Tomo's so proud of her health, she loathes doctors like the plague, so you'd better try persuading her yourself, Shinohara. I'd be very glad if you'd get Dr. Inezawa to come and look at her," he said, playing neatly into Shinohara's hands. Even Yukitomo's feelings had not been untouched by his wife's sudden taking to her bed, and by the picture of her, not seen by himself but described to him by Suga, as she crouched, covered with snow, in the side entrance that snowy evening. The Dr. Inezawa in question, a former classmate and close friend of Shinohara's, was known as one of the very finest physicians in the medical world. Once it was decided that he should come to examine Tomo, her bed was moved to one of the best rooms at the front of the house and Yukitomo with typical ostentation had a fine new set

196

of silk-covered quilts ordered from a well-known store in Nihon-bashi.

"With all this fuss, anybody superstitious would fear the worst," the maids and the foreman said to each other in private.

Their forebodings were justified: Dr. Inezawa's diagnosis was atrophy of the kidneys, so far advanced by now that uremia had already set in. It was impossible in the present state of medicine to do anything for her. She had a month to live at the most.

"She wasn't mistaken after all. Mother knew what was wrong with her," moaned Etsuko when she heard the news from Shino-hara. She had grown used to the idea of her mother as a strong woman who had never been laid up in her life; her mother's words the other day had taken her off her guard, but what on reflection she had dismissed as improbable had now become an unequivocal and pressing reality.

"When we tell Father about the illness, do you think we should tell him what Mother was saying the other day?"

"I think that would be the best time to tell him. Since it's no ordinary occasion he's likely to pay attention for once."

"And to think that Mother's more than ten years younger than Father, too . . . *She* ought to be the one to go on living!" The anxious tears spilled from Etsuko's eyes as she spoke. Although her mother, so rigidly correct all her life, had never let even her daughter presume on her affection, the very fact of her existence had given Etsuko the same sense of security as being in a stout-walled building. The sudden thought of losing that security filled her with unbearable sadness.

When the Shinoharas told Yukitomo that it was doubtful whether Tomo would ever recover, and mentioned to him her request that she be told of her own illness, he nodded and said as though for his own benefit:

"Very well. I'll tell her myself."

Etsuko was looking down at the floor, weeping. Shinohara put a hand on his wife's shoulder, and they left the room. Their place was taken by Suga, who entered without a sound.

"Mrs. Shinohara was crying," she said. "How is the mistress's condition?"

"Not at all good, it seems."

"Why, in what way?" Edging a little closer Suga gazed obliquely at Yukitomo's profile in the dimly lit room. He shifted his gaze to her then turned his face away as though startled by something he saw.

"I'm sure it can't be true. The mistress was always such a strong woman. No—it can't be, it can't . . ."

Yukitomo shook his head without further reply.

An unusually bright winter sun was swelling the buds on the white damson tree in the garden. As she lay in the south-facing room with her head on the pillow Tomo could see the shadow of the venerable tree projected in black by the sunlight, like a painting in Chinese ink, on the translucent white paper of the sliding doors. She could not keep down even soup or milk by now. The very smell of them had become repulsive to her lately. Yet though she ate nothing there was a constant, lurking nausea at the pit of her stomach.

The sliding doors opened smartly and Yukitomo, alone for once, came into the room.

"How are you? A bit better this morning?"

From under heavy lids Tomo looked up at her husband as though at some strange object.

"It's so difficult to tell. What did that Dr. Inezawa say?"

"Apparently he says your kidneys are in a bad way . . . But then there's nothing a good rest can't cure. You've got a tough constitution, after all."

"No!"

She tried to raise her head from the pillow, intending to sit up so that she could talk to her husband. Yukitomo pressed her back. As he placed his hand on the wasted shoulder that he had scarcely touched for dozens of years past, the bone directly beneath the cotton night kimono creaked audibly.

"You don't need to get up. I heard what you said to Etsuko. I'm sure you'll get better, but one's only human and one never knows . . . If there's anything at all you want to say, why don't you say it now? I'll take note of it."

"Very well. It's good of you to say so. I wrote a will so as to be ready in case anything unforeseen should happen. You'll find it, with 'Will' written on it, in the bottom drawer of my cabinet in the room with the altar at the back of the house. I very much want you to know what it says before I die."

She groped beneath the pillow for her key purse and handed it to Yukitomo, watching him steadily as he took it from her. Through all the past decades she had never looked at her husband with such a direct and unwavering gaze. The approach of death had set Tomo free.

Leaving the sickroom Yukitomo went to the room with the Buddhist altar, taking no one with him. It was many years since he had handled the keys to a cabinet personally. Inserting the key in the small hole, he had to turn it one way and the other before it finally opened. Inside, everything was neatly ordered, with a pile of bank deposit books and other documents and, laid on the very top, an envelope with the word "Will" inscribed on it in an ill-formed hand. He took it into the bright light beneath the window and opened it.

The lines of writing were in the same childish hand as the inscription on the envelope. In her labored hand, using old-fashioned, women's language, Tomo wrote of the money that she had amassed without telling Yukitomo. The savings, which came to a considerable sum, all derived originally from the remainder of the money that Yukitomo had handed her thirty years before, when she had gone to Tokyo at his command and brought back the young girl Suga. He had given her two thousand yen and told her to use it as she saw fit. Even after she had paid for Suga's outfit and the expenses of her stay, more than a thousand yen had still remained in her hands. She had intended on her return to draw up the account and return the money to her husband, but seeing his love for the younger Suga she had begun to worry about her own future and had conceived the idea of maintaining her own private fund so as to be ready for the worst, not for her own sake so much as that of Michimasa and Etsuko. With this in mind she had used the money as a basis for her savings, bearing alone over the long years the pain of having to keep a secret from her husband, but none of the money had gone on extravagances for herself. When she was gone, she wrote, she wished the money to be divided among the grandchildren, Suga, Yumi, and others connected with the family.

Again and again, as he read, Yukitomo felt himself reeling before a force more powerful than himself. There was not a word of complaint from Tomo against the outrageous way he had oppressed her: nothing but apology for not having trusted him fully and for always having kept a painful secret from him. Yet the words of apology bore down on his heart more heavily than the strongest protest.

Yukitomo straightened himself up as though to shake off the feeling and strode back along the corridor to Tomo's bedroom.

Tomo lay in bed with her eyes open, in the same position as when he had left.

"Tomo, don't worry—I fully understand what you wrote." His voice was as firm and strong as a young man's. His Kyushu samurai's upbringing had taught him no way to say he was sorry, and this was the closest thing to an apology that he would ever manage.

Tomo looked inquiringly at his face.

"So you forgive me? I'm so grateful."

That night, Tomo drifted into a semi-coma. Even when she was awake her eyes were vacant and she scarcely spoke at all.

Yukitomo cared for the patient, in her new helplessness, as though she were indeed the wife he had cherished faithfully all his days. And the household and relatives, for whom the aged master's word was law, watched over her in a way that did honor at last to his lawful married wife.

It was a night in February when the end was near. That evening, Masamichi's wife Fujie and Yukitomo's niece Toyoko had come to keep watch at the bedside. They had dismissed the nurse and were alone in the sickroom. It was a night of such still, penetrating cold that the charcoal in the brazier seemed to turn to ash almost as soon as it was replenished.

"Toyoko."

Tomo, who had seemed to be dozing, had opened her eyes wide and turned her face towards them on the pillow. Toyoko moved closer as she answered and Fujie hastened to hold her mother-in-law's head for her, fearing that the sudden movement might bring on nausea. But Tomo shook her head irritably to free it from the restraining hand. Shocked at the roughness of the gesture in one who had almost never shown naked feeling before, they stared uncomfortably at the sidelocks, sprinkled with white, falling over the sadly sunken temples. Tomo did not raise her head but she spoke without a break:

"Toyoko, will you go to your uncle and tell him something? Tell him that when I die I want no funeral. Tell him that all he need do is to take my body out to sea at Shinagawa and dump it in the water."

Her eyes were alive and shining with excitement. Their gaze brimmed with feeling of such intensity that they were scarcely recognizable as the placid, leaden-hued eyes that normally looked out from under the heavily drooping lids.

"Really, Aunt—what a thing to say!"

"Whatever makes you say such a thing?"

Toyoko and Fujie protested frantically, but Tomo seemed in a kind of trance and did not hear.

"And go now, please. Otherwise you won't be in time. And you must really tell him. Tell him to dump my body in the sea. Dump it . . ."

Encouraged by the sound of the word "dump," she seemed to utter it with a kind of pleasure.

Since the invalid insisted, Fujie and Toyoko could not but go out into the corridor. In the glance they exchanged as they stood facing each other lay the unspoken feminine complicity of two women who had been married and suffered themselves.

"What do you think? Should we tell him?"

"I think we should, seeing how badly she wants us to."

Both felt a vague dread at the idea of having to shut away inside themselves the accumulation of emotion that Tomo had kept pent up in herself for so long.

"Father, are you still up?" said Fujie as she went into Yuki-tomo's room followed by Toyoko. As usual, Yukitomo was leaning against his back-rest, bathing his eyes with boric-acid solution. Neither Suga nor the children were with him. He veiled the harsh light of his gaze as though in recognition of their service as nurses and said:

"Thank you for helping."

Seating herself, Toyoko in a rapid voice passed on Tomo's

message. She had meant to present it as the delirious nonsense of a sick woman, but when she spoke her voice came out serious and shrill, as though Tomo's spirit had taken possession of her.

The veil cleared instantly from Yukitomo's eyes. The old man's mouth opened as though to say something, then his expression went blank. In the newly bathed, watery eyes, fear stirred as though he had seen a ghost. The next moment, the unnatural effort of the muscles to restore a natural expression wrought havoc with the regular features of his face.

"I could never permit anything so foolish. She will be buried in proper style from this residence. Tell her that, please."

He spoke rapidly in a reproving tone, then turned aside and blew his nose vigorously. His body had suffered the full force of the emotions that his wife had struggled to repress for forty years past. The shock was enough to split his arrogant ego in two.

ACTS OF WORSHIP Seven Stories
Yukio Mishima / Translated by John Bester

These seven consistently interesting stories, each with its own distinctive atmosphere and mood, are a timely reminder of Mishima the consummate writer.

THE SHŌWA ANTHOLOGY
Modern Japanese Short Stories
Edited by Van C. Gessel / Tomone Matsumoto

These 25 superbly translated short stories offer rare and valuable insights into Japanese literature and society. All written in the Shōwa era (1926-1989).

THE HOUSE OF NIRE
Morio Kita / Translated by Dennis Keene

A comic novel that captures the essence of Japanese society while chronicling the lives of the Nire family and their involvement in the family-run mental hospital.

REQUIEM A Novel
Shizuko Gō / Translated by Geraldine Harcourt

A best seller in Japanese, this moving requiem for war victims won the Akutagawa Prize and voiced the feelings of a generation of Japanese women.

A CAT, A MAN, AND TWO WOMEN
Jun'ichiro Tanizaki / Translataed by Paul McCarthy

Lightheartedness and comic realism distinguish this wonderful collection—a novella (the title story) and two shorter pieces. The eminent Tanizaki at his best.

CHILD OF FORTUNE A Novel
Yūko Tsushima / Translated by Geraldine Harcourt

Awarded the Women's Literature Prize, *Child of Fortune* offers a penetrating look at a divorced mother's reluctant struggle against powerful, conformist social pressures.

THE MOTHER OF DREAMS AND OTHER SHORT STORIES
Portrayals of Women in Modern Japanese Fiction

Edited by Makoto Ueda

"[An] appealing anthology." —*Publishers Weekly*

CHILDHOOD YEARS
A Memoir

Jun'ichiro Tanizaki / Translated by Paul McCarthy

The autobiography of Japan's foremost modern novelist.

SALAD ANNIVERSARY

Machi Tawara / Translated by Juliet Winters Carpenter

A poetic search for meaningful love in the 1980's.

THE WAITING YEARS

Fumiko Enchi / Translated by John Bester

"Absorbing, sensitive, and utterly heartrending"
—*Charles Beardsley*

BOTCHAN

Sōseki Natsume / Translated by Alan Turney

A tale about a Japanese Huckleberry Finn.

A HAIKU JOURNEY
Bashō's "The Narrow Road to the Far North" and Selected Haiku.

Bashō Matsuo / Translated by Dorothy Britton

Vivid color photographs help bring Bashō's poetry to life.

THE TWILIGHT YEARS

Sawako Ariyoshi / Translated by Mildred Tahara

"A fascinating and illuminating reading experience." —*Booklist*

THE RIVER KI

Sawako Ariyoshi / Translated by Mildred Tahara

"A powerful novel written with convincing realism."
—*Japan Quarterly*

DISCOVER JAPAN, VOLS. 1 AND 2
Words, Customs, and Concepts

The Japan Culture Institute

Essays and photographs illuminate 200 ideas and customs of Japan.

THE UNFETTERED MIND
Writings of the Zen Master to the Sword Master

Takuan Sōhō / Translated by William Scott Wilson

Philosophy as useful to today's corporate warriors as it was to seventeenth century samurai.

THE JAPANESE THROUGH AMERICAN EYES

Sheila K. Johnson

"Cogent...as skeptical of James Clavell's *Shogun* as it is of William Ouchi's *Theory Z*."—*Publisher's Weekly*

Available only in Japan.

BEYOND NATIONAL BORDERS
Reflections on Japan and the World

Kenichi Ohmae

"[Ohmae is Japan's] only management guru."—*Financial Times*

Available only in Japan.

THE COMPACT CULTURE
The Japanese Tradition of "Smaller is Better"

O-Young Lee / Translated by Robert N. Huey

A long history of skillfully reducing things and concepts to their essentials reveals the essence of the Japanese character and, in part, accounts for Japan's business success.

THE HIDDEN ORDER
Tokyo through the Twentieth Century

Yoshinobu Ashihara

"Mr. Ashihara shows how, without anybody planning it, Japanese architecture has come to express the vitality of Japanese life."
—*Daniel J. Boorstin*